# *miss* MECHANIC

## EMMA HART
*NEW YORK TIMES* BESTSELLING AUTHOR

# *miss* MECHANIC

EMMA HART

NEW YORK TIMES BESTSELLING AUTHOR

*For Ellie.*

*The most patient editor on the planet.*
*And I didn't mention Harry Potter once in this*
*one.*

# 1

## JAMIE

"He was the length of the Amazon River and the girth of the Missouri."

I blinked at my best friend. She could sit there and tell me this about the cock of her latest conquest, but it didn't change the fact he'd stiffed her and not left his number.

And by stiffed, I don't mean their dinner bill.

But, I didn't say that. All I'd get in response would be the reminder that if she was having one-night stands, she didn't want their number.

"That would mean a lot more to me if I knew anything about the *girth* of the Missouri," I replied, wiping my hands on a rag. "There. I filled your oil. I still don't know how you've been driving for eight years and don't know how to change your oil."

Haley grinned, her blue eyes twinkling. "I have you, James. I don't need to know how to change my oil."

I held back the eye roll that wanted to escape.

"One day, I won't be here to do it for you." I unhooked the hood of her Honda and pushed it back down into place with a bang that echoed off the walls.

"You'll always be here. Stop that." She tapped her fingers against the hood and it reverberated throughout my garage. "Thanks, by the way. Twenty bucks?"

I waved my hand at her. "I've never charged you for an oil change and I'm not about to start."

"Well, if a pizza shows up here around six tonight, that's your payment."

"And as always, I will accept without argument." I grinned and closed the drawer of my toolbox.

"Damn right you will." She locked the car, making the lights flash an obnoxious bright-white, and tucked the keys into the pocket of her sweats. "Want a coffee?"

"Need a coffee," I corrected, finally getting the last remnants of oil off my palm. I threw the cloth on top of my huge-ass toolbox and followed her inside to my kitchen.

Haley had already hit the button on the machine that provided my lifeblood when I stepped inside. I pressed my left toes against my right heel and tugged off the Doc Marten boot that encased it, then did the same with the other foot. Kicking them back into the oil-coated garage, I shut the door and pulled off my socks.

"So," she started the moment the coffee machine stopped. "Did you see the ad on

Facebook?"

I leaned against the kitchen counter and folded my arms. "The one for the Chinese-sized sweater or the horrid blackhead facemask?"

She paused. "Well, both, but that wasn't the one I was hinting at."

"I don't do hints, Hales. Spit it out."

She put her mug under the machine. It spat to life, chugging out the coffee like it was a car running on low power. She stayed perfectly silent until the machine squirted out the last of the coffee for the cycle and she'd pulled her mug onto the marble countertop.

"Haley."

"The guy who bought your dad's garage is advertising for a new mechanic."

I almost dropped my mug.

Instead of making a mess I had no desire to clean up, I set it down on the counter and slowly raised my gaze to meet hers. "For real?"

She nodded. "For real. It was an ad in my feed this morning. He renamed it Ryne Garages or something like that. I bet you can search it on Facebook and find it."

I got up, grabbed my laptop from the living room, and took it back into the kitchen. I had it open and loading before I'd even set it on the table, and by the time my ass hit the chair, I'd logged into Windows and was bringing up my Chrome browser.

Facebook loaded immediately.

I typed "Ryne Garages" into the search bar

and waited for it to load. The very first result pulled it up, so I clicked and waited for the page to populate.

The first result held the address I knew so well.

I hovered only a second before I clicked. The cover photo showed the ever-familiar building that was owned by my family for sixty years. Nothing had changed, not really. There'd been a repaint and a new sign put up, but the long-defunct gas station in the front courtyard had been left as I remembered it.

Old, rusting, peeling. Pure, small-town charm of a bygone era.

"You all right, James?"

I took a deep breath. "It's weird. Seeing it with someone else's name on. It's always been ours, but now..."

"It's been a year."

"And now we're in trouble," I said to her. "I get that I'm lucky to live in a house on land we own outright, but if this is open..." I paused and ran my fingers through my hair. "Dad set up in the garage here, but he still doesn't have most of the stuff he needs to keep business smooth. If Rync Garages is open, people will stop coming to us because that will be easier."

Haley grimaced. She knew the truth of my words. The only reason Dad and I had gone so long without working was because the Bell family—us—had been the only mechanics in town for eighty years.

Same building. Same place. Same service.

Until my ex-stepmother's debt had caught up with her and cost us the business.

As Dad had said—losing the business was better than losing our house. We could get jobs. Another house?

The only good thing that had come out of that bullshit mess was the reconciliation of my parents.

"Why don't you apply?" Haley asked after a few minutes of silence. "You need a job, they need a mechanic... You know everyone in town."

I wrinkled my face. "I don't know, Hales. Working in what used to be my family garage? Isn't that weird?"

"Did I or did I not buy you shit paper this week?"

"Asking you for toilet paper wasn't my finest moment," I admitted. "And you didn't have to buy it. I just needed a roll and my parents wouldn't answer their phone."

She waggled her eyebrows.

I pointed my finger at her. "No. Enough. We are not visiting that."

Haley laughed. She waved her hand in the direction of my laptop. "Come on. Just apply. You need a job, and you don't want to drive to get one. It's literally on your doorstep."

I wavered. Little did she know that I'd applied for several jobs in nearby towns over the past few months. I'd been—obviously—unsuccessful, but not because my qualifications lacked.

No.

I was more than qualified.

I was overlooked for one simple reason.

I was a woman.

And I was terrified the same thing would happen again.

I tapped my nails on the trackpad of my laptop.

I knew nothing about the people who'd bought it. Dad had refused to talk about it, and while he's gotten a good price, the divorce had cost him all the money he'd made.

I scrolled down the page to find the job ad Haley had seen. It was a couple of posts down, and I hit 'see more' to read the full offer.

*Mechanic Wanted*

*Mechanic required at Ryne Garages. Located on the corner of Mountain Boulevard, Springbrook. Contact dex@rynegarages.com or call 415-112-1883 for more information and ask for Dexter Ryne.*

Haley leaned over the top of my laptop. "You found it?"

I nodded briskly. "I don't know. Do you not think it's weird? Like, applying for a job in the garage I basically grew up in?"

"Does it feel weird?"

"Yes."

"Just try it. The worst that's going to happen is that they already filled the position or you don't get it."

I stared at her flatly. "There are no other

mechanics in town. Unless someone from outside town applied and got it..."

"Well, then, you have an excellent chance of being accepted, don't you?"

I groaned and rested my head in my hands. "I just...I don't know. It feels really weird to do this."

She smacked her fist against the table, making me jump. "How much money do you have left in your savings account? And that doesn't count the change down the back of the sofa."

Actually, that was a very good question.

I held up one finger and opened online banking.

Ten seconds later, I was staring at a very, very sad bank account.

And I was closing that window because, man, that was depressing.

"We're not going to discuss this," I said, opening Gmail instead.

"You're applying, aren't you?" she asked, a smug smile creeping over her face.

"I'm inquiring."

"Applying."

"Yes! All right, yes. God, I'm applying. There. Are you happy now?" I copied and pasted the email into the 'To' line and attached my resume.

"Ecstatic." She grinned.

I flipped her the bird and, after typing a few lines, sent the email.

---

I turned my key to lock my door. After the telltale click, I checked the handle to make sure and stuffed the keys in my pocket.

Losing the garage a little over a year ago had made me appreciate things a lot more. One of those things was the land we owned on the edge of town. Between my grandparents and my parents, they'd paid it off, and we owned it outright.

The small cottage I called home had been built for a member of staff to live in. It wasn't huge—a living room, a kitchen, a bedroom, and one bathroom—but it was perfect for me. Dad had built the garage next door about ten years ago when it became apparent I was following in his footsteps and not Mom's.

She hadn't been thrilled I'd chosen grease and oil over working with her in her restaurant.

What could I say?

I wasn't really a people person, and there were a lot of people at the restaurant. Cars didn't talk back or complain their chicken was too dry.

No, I was thankful. Thankful that even after my ex-stepmom had put us in debt up to our eyeballs and drained Dad's bank account, we still had a place to live.

Thankful that, twenty-four hours after sending that email, I still hadn't had a response.

Weird, right?

Maybe. But I figured that if I never got a response, I didn't have to suffer the rejection I'd ultimately get because I was the proud owner of a vagina.

Hell, at my last interview, I'd been informed

they didn't have a place on reception open and they were very sorry.

I hadn't even bothered. I'd told them I'd got the wrong building and went home.

I rapped my knuckles against the glass of the back door twice before I pushed it open. "Hello?"

"Jamie? Is that you?" Mom called from another room.

"Are you expecting anyone else for dinner?" I shouted back, closing the door behind me.

"Well," she said, walking into the kitchen with a checked towel slung over her shoulder, "I did see Lou Porter earlier today..."

I pointed my finger at her. "Don't you dare. I am not dating Stuart again."

She burst into laughter, the melodic sound ringing through the room. "Don't worry, honey. I don't want you to date Stuart either."

I blew out a long breath and slipped onto a stool at the kitchen island. "Thank God for that. If I have to listen to another rendition of his ill-fated relationship with his bitch ex, I'm going to scoop out my eardrums with a bent paperclip."

"That's more visual than I'd hoped for," Mom said, whisking a full chicken out of the oven. She set it on the side in one swift movement, kicked the oven door shut, and threw the oven mitt over her left shoulder.

Between that and the tea towel, she looked every bit the housewife. The apron didn't help, either...

"You're welcome. Where's Dad?"

She walked to the fridge as steam rose from the chicken. "He's in the garage, tinkering with that old Chevy truck he's been playing with. I think he's almost to the root of the problem." She pulled out a bottle of wine and held it up as if to ask me if I wanted it.

I nodded.

She slid it over to me along with a corkscrew.

I got to work.

"Why do you ask? Did you need him?"

"No," I said, working the corkscrew. "I wanted to talk to you about something."

Mom set two wine glasses in front of me and leveled me with her blue eyes. "Which is?"

"I applied for a job today."

"Where?"

I eked out the cork. "The garage that used to be ours."

"Hooooooooey." Mom blew out a long breath as she grabbed the neck of the bottle and poured two pathetic excuses for glasses of wine.

She paused, bottle still in hand, and topped up both glasses.

Well, that said a lot about what she thought about what I'd said.

Mom was a lady—from wine to hemlines, if you could make her British, she'd be a damn royal with all her manners and etiquette.

The fact she'd just poured a whole damn glass of wine... Well.

She grabbed hers and took a big mouthful. Her cheeks puffed out as she held it in her mouth before swallowing it. "That's...unexpected."

"No kidding. Haley saw the ad on Facebook and told me when I did her oil yesterday. They need a new mechanic, and it's not like I have anything to lose."

A change from my thoughts of yesterday, I know, but whatever.

I reserve the right to change my mind a hundred times a day.

I am a woman.

"You're right," Mom said, setting down her glass. "Don't you worry that it'll be weird?"

"Honestly, I worry more that I'll be dismissed because I'm a woman," I replied softly. "That's usually the way it goes."

She turned. Her expression was gentle—her eyes understanding without pitying the way only a mom's eyes could express. "I know, honey. But you can do this. You might have to prove yourself—a fact I believe is bullshit, by the way—but you can."

"I shouldn't have to prove myself. I have the experience. I have the qualifications. Why isn't that good enough just because I wear a bra and turn into a demi-demon once a month?"

"Because." She stopped as if she didn't know herself. She reached for her glass and cradled it against her chest.

The timer on the stove went off.

She sipped quickly and put the glass down, then grabbed the pan and drained the potatoes, somehow turning off the stove at the same time.

"Because what?" I asked, spinning the stem of my glass between my finger and thumb.

Mom sighed as she turned off the veggies and pulled the boiling pan from the heat. "Because, Jamie," she said softly, "You will always be second best in your industry. You will always be chasing the lights as long as you stick with it."

Her words rang true, but... "You want me to work with you."

She turned. "I want you to do what makes you happy, Jamie. I would love for you to work with me, but I know cars are your passion. I'm terrified that these constant rejections will hurt you."

"I'm good enough, damn it!" I slammed my fist against the table and instantly regretted it. Wasn't that what she was talking about?

"I know that." Mom's voice was still soft, even as she began the process of mashing the potatoes. "But others don't, and I don't want anyone to dim your passion, baby girl."

"My passion doesn't depend upon the acceptance of other people. It never has, and it never will. I won't stop wanting to be the best I can be just because someone else decides I'm not good enough."

"I'm so thankful you have such a positive outlook." She pulled plates from the cupboard. "But one day, it might happen. Someone might make you believe you aren't good enough, and I worry you aren't prepared for that."

"Mom." I met her eyes. "I've spent the last several months being rejected for jobs in a field

I'm more than qualified in because I'm a woman. I'm twenty-six-years-old and can't date because I can fit a spare tire quicker than my date. I've loved what I do longer than I can remember. Someone's opinion will not change that."

The front door slammed before she could reply.

"What's for dinner?" Dad asked, strolling into the kitchen in a waft of motor oil and fresh air. The strangest mix known to man, but oddly comforting.

"Chicken, mashed potatoes, and veggies," Mom replied.

"What are we talking about?" He dragged his two-hundred-and-fifty-pound frame over to the sink and squirted bright purple soap into his palms.

"Assholes writing me off," I cut right to the chase.

He snorted.

Mom sighed. "Not at all. I'm simply worried that someone, somewhere, will make her question her worth."

Dad shut off the tap and pulled the towel off her shoulder. "Jamie? Question her worth? As what? A person or a mechanic?"

"Right now...Mechanic."

Dad blinked at her, then turned his salt-and-pepper stubble-dotted face toward me. "Sunshine, if they do, throw your wrench in their face. I'll pay your bail."

I grinned. "While you're in such a good mood,

I applied for a job at the old garage."

He pulled a beer from the fridge. Without blinking, he replied, "Well, he's a fucking idiot if he doesn't hire you, sunshine."

I couldn't agree more.

# 2

## JAMIE

*To: Jamie-bell@gmail.com*
*From: dex@rynegarages.com*
*Subject: RE: Job Application*

*Jamie,*
*Apologies for the late reply. If you're free, I can see you at 11.30 today for an interview.*
*Please bring ID, a hard copy of your resume, and a certification of your qualifications.*
*Best,*
*Dexter Ryne*

*To: dex@rynegarages.com*
*From: Jamie-bell@gmail.com*
*Subject: RE: Job Application*

*Mr. Ryne,*
*Thank you for your response. I'll be at your garage just before 11.30 today with your requested materials.*

*Many thanks,*
*Jamie*

---

I pulled into the courtyard of Ryne Garages. Shivers crept down my spine as goosebumps trickled over my skin. It just felt wrong—all of it.

It shouldn't have a sign that read Ryne Garages. It should have been Bell Garages. The walls should have been white and not yellow. The plant outside the front door should have been a cactus and not...whatever the hell that mess was.

It was easy to pick.

It was everything that was wrong with my family's name not being in lights over this garage.

Whatever.

I'd look past it, walk in, and get this interview over and done with. I had to. Even if my mom's words constantly rang in my mind.

What if my passion was killed?

I was so sure it wouldn't be. Some things were so deeply embedded in one's soul there was no pulling them out—like a staple gun to the butt—and I knew cars were that for me.

They were fucking everything. Life and soul and oxygen. I loved them more than I knew how to love anything. It was so natural to me.

But what if someone possessed the power to break that?

It was a deep and irrational fear, but a legitimate one all the same.

And now, I was faced with it. It was right in front of me. A big-ass threat I didn't know if I was mentally equipped to deal with.

I pulled my keys from the ignition.

No, I was equipped. I was ready. I'd lived my life with a refusal to make anyone make me feel like I was worth less than I knew I was, and I wasn't going to change that now.

I was Jamie Fucking Bell. I was a mechanic's daughter. I'd once painted a car with motor oil on an order form at the age of three, and I'd once written an English essay while cross-legged on the hood of a '69 Mustang that was being restored for my uncle.

There wasn't a damn thing anyone could teach me about a car that I didn't already know.

I bled motor oil. I breathed the rancid air of gas. And I fought every day against the discrimination of that.

And I was tired of people putting me down because I had a pair of boobs.

I got out of my car and slammed the door behind me. Something that would make my father cringe—two years restoring the aforementioned '69 Mustang was a proud moment of his, and although the teal-blue car had always been destined for me, it didn't mean he liked when I "hurt that baby."

I got it, but I was fired up.

I was ready for this interview, and I sure as fucking hell wasn't going to walk out without proving to this guy I was more than worthy of his job.

---

I slowly pushed open the door to the garage and stepped into the uncomfortably familiar reception area. A bell over the door dinged, and when I looked up, I saw a tiny, brass bell—much smaller than the one my grandfather had installed years ago.

The noise was much nicer, that was for sure.

I smoothed my hands over my dress as I approached the counter. There was crashing at the back, followed by a rough grunt of a cuss word.

A smile tugged at my lips as I cast my gaze around the room. It was all so clean and tidy. There was a scarlet-red sofa beneath the windows, and a mahogany coffee table scattered with magazines stood just in front of it. A large, leafy plant occupied the corner, its leaves just tickling the corner of a retro car sales poster pinned to the wall.

"Jesus," came a low mutter from behind me.

I turned with a start, my hands coming together silently in front of my stomach.

The door behind the counter shut, and when I blinked, I was able to focus on the guy standing in front of me.

Who was, quite possibly, the most handsome guy I'd seen in a long-ass time.

My gaze wandered over him. Navy blue

overalls covered his legs, and he'd tied the sleeves at his waist. A white t-shirt hugged an obviously muscular body, and everything from his large hands to his toned biceps were splattered with oil and grease.

I lifted my gaze another couple inches higher. To his face. To the five o'clock shadow that dotted his jaw. Full lips. Bright-blue eyes surrounded by unfairly thick, dark eyelashes. And a head full of hair the exact same shade of brown as his lashes.

He wiped at his forehead, pushing the hair from his eyes—and swiping oil across his skin. "Sorry about that. Slipped on some water and kicked the corner of a toolbox." He grimaced. "What can I do for you, darlin'?"

"I have an appointment with Dexter Ryne?"

He held out his hands. "You're looking at him."

Well, that was easy.

"I'm Jamie Bell." I offered my hand over the counter.

Dexter Ryne froze. Slowly, his gaze moved over my face as if he were drawing a sketch in the air with his eyes, taking in every inch of me. Then, it moved to my hand.

*Here we go again...*

I let my hand fall back to my side and suppressed a sigh. "You emailed me yesterday? About the interview? I have my resume right here." I pulled it out of my unzipped purse and set it on the counter between us.

He dropped his attention to that, blinked, and shook his head. "Jamie Bell. Sure. But...You know this is for a job out back, right?" He jerked his thumb over his shoulder.

"I'm not in the habit of applying for jobs I'm not qualified to do, Mr. Ryne," I replied sweetly. "I'm fully aware of that fact."

"It's Dex. Mr. Ryne is my father...and my grandfather." He eyed me speculatively, then snatched up my resume. "I wasn't aware women worked as mechanics."

"Then I'm thrilled I've been able to enlighten you that we exist." I tried to stay sweet, but I couldn't. A hint of sarcasm tinged my words.

He glanced up, raising one eyebrow, but said nothing. Instead, he left me standing here while he scanned my resume.

"This doesn't say you're a woman," he said, putting it back down.

"Do you say you're a man on your resume?"

"My name gives it away."

"I'll be sure to inform my parents they should have given me a name that hinted more at my gender," I replied dryly.

His lips twitched, but whatever smile was forming, he fought against. "I'm not sure I'm a fan of your attitude."

I looked him dead in the eye and said, "Then we have something in common because I don't much like yours."

Both his eyebrows shot up. "What experience do you have?"

"I worked weekends from fourteen until I graduated. Became an apprentice the next day, and worked up until a year ago. I've since been working from home."

"Why?"

"My father had to sell his garage." I folded my arms across my chest. "I struggled to get work."

Would he figure it out?

Nothing that looked like recognition flitted across his expression, so the answer was probably no.

"Right." Short and sharp, I knew he didn't buy the truth he was being fed.

Prejudice. It was written all over him. I could hear it in his words, I could sense it in the way he held himself, and I could see it in his eyes when he looked at me.

The slightly frizzy-haired brunette in the tailored black dress and high heels, wearing the light, gray sweater and carrying the Coach purse.

I didn't look like I belonged in a garage at all. The only thing that gave it away was my unpolished, trimmed nails.

What? You couldn't fit a new gearbox if you had talons on the ends of your fingers, and nothing frustrated me more than chipped polish after working.

Silence held between us for a minute. Dex, as he wanted to be called, said nothing. He didn't even stare at me. He looked—glared—at my resume. The battle he fought was obvious.

He was new to town, and Facebook showed he'd been advertising for two weeks.

There was nobody nearby who was a mechanic.

I was his first and only application.

I leaned against the counter, resting my fingers against its edge. "Mr. Ryne—"

"Is my father," he replied.

Well, that much was for sure. His politeness made me want to refer to him as "son," never mind mister. And he was definitely older than me.

"Dex," I said, adding extra emphasis. "If you have an issue with hiring me, say so right now so I can stop wasting my time with this conversation."

"What makes you think I have an issue with you?"

Flatly, I stared at him. "I'm a woman."

He waved his hand, slapping my resume down off the counter. The sheets scattered to the floor. "Never worked with one that wasn't on reception. Never come across one that didn't belong on reception."

My heels tapped against the linoleum as I walked around the counter and, for the second time, held out my hand. "Pleasure to meet you, Dexter Ryne. My name is Jamie Bell, and I most definitely do not belong on reception."

Once again, he glanced at my hand. He held his up. "Wouldn't want to mess up your pretty dress, darlin'."

I snatched his hand out of the air and dragged it down between us, shaking it firmly. Eyes still on his, I said, "A little oil doesn't bother me, darlin'."

He held my hand for a moment, our gazes locked, before he ground out, "I guess you better let yourself out the back, then." He let go of my hand, then leaned over the counter and peered down at my heels. "Sorry, I don't have another pair of shoes for you to wear."

"No bother." I unhooked the bar-like counter and stepped to within inches of his body. "I've changed tires in higher heels than these."

I couldn't tell if he was impressed or pissed at my mouth. And I didn't care.

If Dex Ryne was going to come into my town and run his mouth at me, I was going to teach him a thing or two about small-town, Southern girls.

I was sweet as pie.

Until you pissed me off.

Then...

Well, then, I'd shut you down quicker than a hooker shut down a guy after a free blowie.

"Are we going?" I asked when he didn't move.

He turned and yanked the door open. It slammed back against the stopper installed on the floor and swung right back to closed.

I stilled and let out a sigh.

But hey—this was closer than I'd ever been before.

I pulled open the door. Immediately, I was hit with the rich scent of fuel and oil. Of metal and grease.

Of everything I was comfortable with.

Not caring at all, I took the step down onto the workshop floor and looked around.

It hadn't changed a bit.

No matter what they'd done to the outside, the inside was the same. The tool racks commanded the same wall. The work counters commanded the same, and the doors to the bathroom and staff room hadn't been replaced.

They'd re-painted everything, including the red floor, but it had all been futile. Tools and oil and paint covered every surface. It was every inch the garage it was the day we sold it.

It even had Mrs. Hawkins' little Ford in the corner. The damn car was always in for something or another—we'd even 'fixed' her lack of fuel issue before.

In a weird way, it was good to see that some things didn't change.

It was definitely strange to see someone else's things here, though. Almost disconcerting not to look in the far corner and see my father's beloved tool unit and the old oil sign that used to hang above it. Now, that corner was bare.

I took a deep breath and let it out slowly.

Dex eyed me speculatively—almost cruelly, actually. There was a dark glint in his gaze that sent a shiver down my spine.

I looked out of place right now, but properly dressed, I'd be home.

"This is it," he said, waving his arm around the garage. Slowly, he gave me the tour. Showed me where everything was, and I hummed as if it was all unfamiliar to me.

When it was done, I rested my hand against the side of a toolbox. "You look like you'd rather be anyone else."

"I'd rather you be a man," he said coolly.

"Does it matter? I'm just as qualified as any other person would be." I folded my arms across my chest, and the strap of my purse cut into the crook of my elbow. "There's nothing any man could do that I can't."

"I'll need to see your qualifications."

"You'll have to find the certification in the mess you made of my resume," I ground out.

He grunted and turned on the balls of his feet, going back to the reception area.

Screw this. Never mind me being a woman—this man was insufferable. He was beyond sexist and prejudiced. I'd never met anyone quite like it.

What I should have done was told him thanks, but no thanks.

What I wanted to do was prove him wrong.

I joined him in the reception with one last, longing glance into the garage. He'd picked up all the sheets of paper and was sorting them on the desk.

"Did you find them?" I asked.

He grunted again.

Oh, boy. I'd found proof that cavemen did still exist.

I held out my hand for the resume.

Bright blue eyes found mine, and he handed it over. "I'm gonna level with you, Ms. Bell—"

"Jamie."

"—This isn't going to work. It's not because

you're not qualified. You are. But honestly, I'm not comfortable working with a woman in my garage."

My lips pursed as he continued speaking.

"While you're suitably qualified, I question whether or not you're strong enough for most of the tasks required."

Don't speak, Jamie. Take it and leave.

"I'm sorry, but thank you for coming in anyway."

Then, the jerk had the audacity to smile at me. Fucking smile.

"See, all I heard there was a bunch of excuses about why you can't have a woman in your garage." The words left my mouth before I could stop them.

Dex faltered, his smile dropping. "I'm sorry?"

"I don't believe you at all." I leaned against the counter. "I think you're afraid I'll go back there and prove you and your stupid, outdated ideas wrong. I think you're worried I'll be a better mechanic than you are."

His eyebrows shot up. Amusement flashed in his eyes, but it was the wry curve of his lips as they formed a smirk that said I'd hit a home run with that. "Very astute, Jamie. And completely incorrect."

"So, why not hire me? If you're not afraid of being proven wrong, what do you have to lose? Apart from a bit of an apparently over-sized ego, of course."

He laughed and folded his muscular arms. He

leaned against the doorframe, the ghost of the laugh on his lips, and studied me. "Are you really trying to argue your way into this job?"

"No. I'm trying to get to the root of the real reason you don't want a woman in your workshop, and all I've got is that you're genuinely afraid that I'll be too damn good."

All right. I was totally tooting my own horn but damn it. I was damn good at my job. I'd learned from the best, from two generations of mechanics, and I wasn't going to allow him to demean me just because I made him uncomfortable.

Dex rubbed his hand over his chin. His stare was intense, but I held his gaze. I wasn't going to back down.

If he thought I was, he was very much mistaken.

"All right." He dropped his arms and walked over to me. "I'll make you deal, darlin'."

I waited.

His lips quirked. "Since you're so insistent, I'll give you three weeks. If, at the end of three weeks, you've proven me wrong and you can hack it, I'll give you a permanent job."

When he paused, I said, "What's the catch?"

Resting his forearms on the counter, he leaned forward, smirk still in place. "If I don't think you've done enough, your job will be on reception."

I glared at him.

"Of course," he said, standing up with a shit-eatingly smug glint in his eye, "If you don't think you can prove how good you are in three weeks, you don't have to accept."

The bastard had taken my words, flipped them, and thrown them right back at me.

# 3

## DEX

Jamie Bell stepped toward the counter. With her stunningly bright blue eyes fixed on mine, she said, "I won't need three weeks."

Her confidence was astounding. She was just shy of arrogant. She had the kind of confidence that made you stop and stare, just in case she really was as good as she said she was.

Was she?

A part of me wanted her to accept my offer.

A part of me wanted to see if her confidence wasn't unfounded—if it had a real basis.

A part of me wanted her to say yes just so I could stare at her a little fucking longer.

When I'd said I didn't know women were mechanics—it was a lie. I meant women like *her* weren't mechanics. Women with eyelashes that were so curved they tickled her skin weren't. Women who had full lips that would be attractive with or without lipstick weren't.

The women I knew who were mechanics didn't wear high heels and dresses that hugged every motherfucking sinful curve of their body.

I only knew two women, but my point remained.

Jamie Bell was a fucking enigma. One I wanted in my garage and the fuck away from it. I couldn't compute this...siren...with one who would be comfortable wearing sneakers and overalls. This woman who had perfectly fixed makeup and had her face surrounded by slightly frizzy hair wouldn't fit if she were covered in oil.

But, fuck. Between her mouth—that sassy, unfiltered mouth that called me on the most pathetic excuses of my life—and her body, I was intrigued.

She was hot as fuck. And no doubt a force to be reckoned with if you pushed her hard enough.

And call me a fucking sadist, but I wanted to push her.

I wanted to push her to the limit. Find her breaking point. Make her push and push until she snapped on me.

She laid her hand on the top of the counter. Her gaze never wavered.

The girl had balls.

"You've got a deal, Dexter Ryne," she said firmly. "And I'm gonna make you eat your words."

I leaned forward, right over the counter until there were mere inches between us. "I look forward to you eating your own, darlin'."

"I don't eat my words." She straightened. "I

eat the souls of sexist asses like you."

"Careful." My lips twitched. "As of right now, I'm your boss."

She stared at me, a flat, hard stare that would have made a lesser man shiver.

Instead, my lips broke into a full-fledged smirk. "Monday morning. Be here at seven-thirty. In...more suitable attire." I ran my gaze up and down her curvaceous body, just to make my point clear.

She tugged her purse strap up over her shoulder. "I'll see you then."

Then, she turned on her heel and left, leaving the door to swing shut after it. It slammed back into the frame, the sound echoing through the empty reception, and I let go of a low chuckle.

Man, she was a fucking firecracker.

I wasn't worried she'd prove me wrong. Fuck no—I wasn't worried at all. I wanted her to prove me damn wrong.

She just didn't look like the kind of girl who could hack it. And her resume stating that she worked for her father for her entire life didn't exactly lend credence to her ability to do this jo.

For all I knew, Jamie Bell had had it easy for her entire life.

That was about to change.

Even if, at the start, I had to treat her like the idiot she assumed I thought she was.

I couldn't fucking wait.

"You hired someone yet?" Pops slammed his half-empty coffee mug down on the table and used his walking stick to sit himself on the sofa.

"Just today," I replied, not looking up from my phone.

He reached over and snatched it out of my hands. "Look at me when I'm talkin' to ya, boy."

I took a deep breath and turned to face him. "Just today," I repeated.

"Tell me about him," he demanded gruffly. "And pass me that damn coffee."

I hid my smile as I picked up the mug and handed it to him.

He was brash and harsh, but beneath that demeanor, he was a big old fucking softie. Not that I ever told him that—that was only permitted on birthdays.

"Thanks." He sipped, then set the mug on his knee. "Well? Tell me about your new hire."

"It's a woman."

Pops froze, then slowly slid his gaze over to meet mine with the tiniest jerk of his head. "You hired a woman?"

I held my hands up. "She challenged me. It pissed me off. I challenged her right back."

Letting go of his stick, he pinched the bridge of his nose. "This is business, Dex. Not a means to get yourself laid."

"Jesus Christ," I muttered. "She's hot, but sleeping with her would give me a headache. She runs her mouth far too much for that."

Pops snorted. "So did your grandma. Then I married her."

"Well, I'm not that stupid."

Another snort. "Tell me about her. She qualified? She tell you where to stick your stupid-ass opinions?"

My lips thinned. "You think I'd hire someone if she wasn't qualified?"

"If it got you laid, I think you'd consider it. In fact, I know you would."

"I don't need to hire some mouthy, overconfident chick to get laid."

Pops chuckled. "She told you where to stick it."

"A few times," I admitted. Begrudgingly. "You know how I feel about women out the back. The last time we tried to hire one she couldn't pick up a goddamn tire."

"And that's because you were more interested in screwing her than anything else." He waved his wrinkled finger in my face. "She wasn't qualified. Tell me about this new lady."

He was so fucking polite. Sometimes.

"She's more than qualified." I grabbed my beer from the table and settled back, my eyes staring in the direction of the TV and the car restoration show I'd been watching. Unfocused on it, I continued. "She worked weekends as a teen, picked up an apprenticeship the day after she graduated, and worked full-time ever since. Stopped a year ago when her dad was forced to sell the family garage."

"So, what's your damn problem?" Pops snapped. "She paint her nails?"

I shot him a dark look. "*Over*confident. She thinks she's better than she is."

"You hired her off a challenge. She obviously thinks she's better than you."

"She's wrong."

"And you criticize her for being overconfident." He laughed.

"Criticize who?" my great aunt, Greta, asked as she hobbled into the room, clutching a vase in her hands. Her bright blue gaze darted between the two of us. "Well? Spit it out, boy."

I fucking hated it when they called me that, but they were creatures of habit. Really fucking old ones.

"His new employee," Pops said, watching the TV. "They're doing that wrong." He waved his finger.

"That took you long enough," Greta said. "Where'd you find 'em?"

"She walked into reception this morning," I answered.

"Then proceeded to shut his ass up," Pops chuckled. "I'm gonna need the CCTV of that."

I gave him another dark look.

"Ooooh," Greta trilled. She set down the vase and pointed at me. "She under your skin, boy."

"I don't know her," I shot back. "But if by 'her' you mean her hideous confidence and sassy attitude, then sure, she is."

She laughed. Loud and long. "Oh, look. You

metcha match."

I wished she would talk like a normal person.

"Don't go there," I warned.

"Hideous confidence and sassy attitude," she mused, stroking her chin. "Gosh, Eddie, do we know anyone like that?"

Pops smirked, looking at me. "Sure don't, Gretie."

They were referring to my sister. The only woman who'd ever been able to kick me in the balls and keep the damn things tucked up in my stomach until she'd left.

I leaned back on the sofa and swigged my beer. "I don't know why I come here for dinner."

"'Cause you can't cook," Greta said, wiping her hands on her apron. "And you secretly like it when I torture you."

Well, she was right on the first.

The second... Not so much.

# 4

## JAMIE

"That," Haley said, hand clasped around a bottle of water, "Is the stupidest thing you've ever done."

I threw my hands in the air. "What did you expect me to do? Kow-tow to his fucked up sexism?"

"Politely thank him for his time and leave!"

I shook my head. "No. Honestly, Hales, I've never met such a fucking asshole in my life. He wasn't worried about me being strong enough to do the job. He's worried I'd show him up."

"Has anyone ever told you that your confidence could be mistaken for arrogance?"

"Yes. You. All the time." I huffed and hit the button on the treadmill to take the incline up a level. I wasn't a runner, so I walked practically a ninety-degree angle to make up for it. "Seriously, it was all over him. Let's face it—I'm more than qualified, and he's so ass-backward in his belief of where I belong as a poor little woman that it was unbearable."

"So, your fix to that is to work with him? With your temper?" She raised her eyebrow and moved to a slow jog. "Do you really think it's a good idea?"

"I never claimed it was a good idea," I retorted. "I think it's a terrible idea, but I have this insatiable need to prove him wrong."

"Since when did you ever care about proving someone—much less a man—wrong?"

She had a point. "Well, yesterday morning."

Haley rolled her eyes and took a sip of her water. "You don't want this job, James. You've walked away from these interviews a hundred times before. This is ridiculous."

I wished she'd stop talking sense. She was making me start to regret my choice.

"I know it's ridiculous. You don't have to keep telling me." I huffed and swigged my water. "I just... There's something about him that tells me he needs his smugness smacking off his face."

"So, punch him instead of work for him."

"No. It'll be far more satisfying when I show him I'm not a delicate fucking flower."

"Ah, yes. Let me send that to whoever is heading up the feminist movement these days. Sounds like you just gave them a new slogan."

I shot her a withering look. "You're such an asshole. Honestly, you should take your car to the garage and talk to him. I bet you'd see exactly what I mean."

She slowed the treadmill to a walk. "Why would I take my car in there? You're going on like he's your sworn enemy, and now you're telling me to take my custom to him!"

"You twist my words, Haley Allen."

Her grin stretched across her entire face. "I know. I'm trying to catch you out. You're really going to work with a guy you hate?"

"I don't hate Dex. I don't know enough about him to hate him, but from the first impression, he's probably going to be a permanent addition to my shit list."

"Oooh, your shit list. What are you going to do?"

"Bitch and whine every night to some unlucky soul who gets to call herself my best friend."

"Oh boy," she said dryly. "I didn't pull the short straw at all."

I turned to look at her. "You know, I forget. Who made me apply for this job in the first place?"

She said nothing. She simply flipped me the bird, looking straight ahead, and put her earbuds in her ears.

I laughed to myself.

She was such a tool.

---

Monday morning rolled around all too quickly. After having the weekend to sleep on things and several messages from Haley about how stupid I was, all my six a.m. alarm did was wake me to the reality that I was about to work for a total asshole.

What was I doing?

I valued myself more than this.

I was worth more than proving myself to an egotistical little man because he didn't think I was worth it.

But I couldn't stop. I couldn't tear myself away from the need to do this.

Was it because, on the surface, I was attracted to him? Or because he just made me want to wipe that stupid, sexy, smug smirk off his goddamn face?

Jesus, I didn't even know. Holy shit. I was in trouble.

I wasn't doing this because I wanted to. I was doing it because I felt like I had to. I had to be the one to smash his stupid little ideals into pieces.

What was wrong with me?

I decided not to answer that and headed for the shower instead. I hadn't exactly slept well last night, but the hot water beat down on me and washed away a lot of the aches that plagued my shoulders.

Ten minutes later, I emerged from my bathroom wrapped in towels and headed back into my room. I'd laid out a simple tank top and shorts set the night before. I didn't particularly care about either item and actually, I was sure the shorts had an oil stain on the butt pocket.

I changed, carefully balancing the towel on my hair. My unruly, frizzy curls were currently jailed in it, and I wanted to keep it that way as long as possible.

Another ten minutes passed while I dressed and applied minimal makeup. Judging by our initial meeting, I expected to be thrown onto reception and customer service within hours of me starting today. If that was the case, I needed to look somewhat presentable, no matter what Dex said about makeup and shit.

I even put on the goddamn red lipstick.

Just to prove I could fix cars while wearing it.

God, now I was point-scoring.

I shook my head at myself and released my mop of hair from the towel. It was a hot mess as it tumbled in wet curls over my shoulders, and I had to grit my teeth to get through the knotty mess it was.

Thank God for the wide-toothed comb. It made its way through the fluff until I was able to whisk it all into a messy bun on top of my head.

Then, I looked in the mirror, and let out a long, heavy breath.

I was ready for this. I was ready to drive to Ryne Garages and begin the task of proving Dex wrong.

Was I?

I'd been so determined—until Haley had told me how stupid the idea was. How my self-worth had never been defined by anyone else until I saw him.

She was right.

It was stupid.

My self-worth was defined by nobody other

than me—and that wouldn't change. Whether or not Dexter Ryne believed I was good enough to be a mechanic in his garage was nothing more than his opinion, and since opinions were usually closer to assholes than anything else, I didn't care what he thought.

I just cared that, for a second, I made him think something else.

And I didn't know why I cared. I had no reason to care. His prejudice would not change just because I, one person, proved him wrong.

Still. I'd never claimed to be this generation's Einstein.

I grabbed all my things together and headed out of the door and to my car. She rumbled to life when I turned the key in the ignition, and I took a deep breath and pulled away from my house.

Stones crunched beneath the tires as I followed the long, makeshift drive that connected the path to my house to the main one to my parents'. As soon as I turned onto the main drive, it was mere seconds until I was out onto the main road and driving in the direction of the garage.

I'd driven it so many times I didn't pay any attention. I knew the stores I'd pass. I knew what the trees on Main Street looked like as they turned to fall colors and wilted all over the sidewalk. I knew what it looked like to pass the bigger houses on the opposite side of town.

What it looked like to roll just slightly off the beaten track to where the garage sat.

I pulled into the same spot I did for my

interview and parked. Everything inside shut off with one turn of the key, and I stayed still for a moment.

I had to get myself together.

Now.

I grabbed my stuff from the passenger side and got out before I turned into a huge chicken. Locking my car, I stuffed the keys into my purse and walked toward the garage.

There were no lights. I tried the front door, but it was locked, and I pursed my lips.

"Jamie?"

I jumped, clutching my purse close to me.

A low chuckle sounded. "Round the back."

Slowly, I edged back toward my car and where the back door to the garage was. Why didn't I think of that? That was always how we'd entered. I guessed my uncertainty had gotten the better of me.

I'd forgotten that entrance ever existed.

The silhouette of Dex filled the doorway until my eyes adjusted to the dim light of the fall morning and I could make him out.

Boy, I was not looking forward to daylight savings next week.

"Dex?"

"Did I scare you?"

"Like a lamb scares a lion," I replied, walking toward him.

He didn't step out of the door—he only flattened himself against the frame, meaning I had to turn sideways to slide past him. Barely a breath of air would have been able to go between us, but at least we didn't touch.

"You're early," he noted.

"Would you prefer if I were late?" I shot over my shoulder, walking into the staff area and dumping my purse on the sofa.

"I'd prefer you be on time."

Now, he was taking the piss.

"I'll take that into consideration. If I'm ever late, know that it was because I was doing my best to get here exactly on time."

"We're beginning this trial on good terms, I see."

I turned, ready to shoot him down, but all I saw was a wolfish grin that glinted in his eyes. "It's first thing on a Monday. You'll learn that I don't do sarcasm this early."

"Ironic, considering the snark you just sent my way."

"I'm sorry—I meant to say I don't take sarcasm from other people on a Monday unless they have a murder wish."

Dex burst into laughter and locked the door I'd just walked through. "Just on a Monday? I admit to having limited experience in your presence, but I'd consider you a potential murderer any day of the week."

I leveled my gaze on him. "And you're in a building full of potential murder weapons."

"I'll take my chances."

"They're weak."

"I'm strong and scrappy—I could fight you off,

darlin'."

"I'm a mean hand at Chinese throwing stars," I warned him. Still wasn't sure how I'd acquired that skill...

He grinned. "Good thing I don't have any of those stashed in here."

"Wrenches spin the same way."

He faltered. "Point well made. From now on, though, watch your mouth. I'm your boss."

"Did I scare you?"

"Into thinking I hired a psychopath? Absolutely. Of a woman who wears lipstick to fix cars? Not really." He tossed a clipboard my way. It landed with a clatter at my feet. "I'm starting you off easy."

I bent to retrieve it. "So kind of you."

"Mrs. Hawkins' Ford needs an oil change, spark plugs replaced, and her two front tires changed." He hesitated. "That's the dark blue, three-door disaster in the back corner."

"No, stop that," I snapped back. "I thought it was that shiny as hell, black Dodge Ram to my left."

Dex blinked his blue eyes at me for a moment. "Do you have a switch for that attitude? Does coffee turn it off?"

"No, but it gives me the ability to pretend to like people."

He moved back toward the staffroom. "Cream and sugar?"

"Yes, and one, please." I flashed him an almost-sincere smile.

"Damn, that was almost a real one." His laughter followed him into the room—and I did, too.

I opened up my purse and pulled out the overalls I'd scrunched into a tiny ball. Creases made no difference when they'd be hidden by oil in mere minutes of being under a hood.

I kicked off my combat boots, sat down, and shoved my legs in the leg-holes.

Dex glanced over his shoulder, his eyes lingering on my shoes in front of me.

When he didn't say anything, I did. "Yes?"

He peered back at me for a moment before returning his attention to the coffee machine. "I half-expected you to show up in those heels you wore to the interview."

I bit my tongue, holding back a retort for half a second. "If you'd like me to, it's not a problem. I've changed a tire in higher heels before."

"Now, that's something I'd like to see."

"It's something I'd like to forget," I admitted, standing and zipping the overalls to beneath my boobs. Starting to roll the sleeves, I continued, "My mom was driving me to dinner with a few friends and we saw old Mr. Hooter on the side of the road with a flat. His cell wasn't working. Neither were ours because we were out of range. I wasn't exactly dressed for tire-changing, and we'll just say he enjoyed the view."

He snorted. "Now I definitely want a recreation."

I leveled a flat stare at the back of his head.

Not only was he sexist, but he was apparently a perv.

Or attracted to me.

I preferred the former option.

A perv, I could deal with. A guy as hot as him? Not so much.

Although, his mouth shut that shit down pretty quick... Probably just like mine did.

Thank God.

I'd have to go to pray for small mercies, aka sarcasm, this weekend.

Ugh... My mom was going to love dragging me to church.

# 5

## JAMIE

"Could you get that?" Dex asked from beneath the Dodge Ram.

He was lucky I'd just finished putting the new front tire on Mrs. Hawkins' Ford, or I'd have told him the answer was no.

Instead, I sighed and headed for the ringing phone.

I picked it up and put it to my ear with a glance through the closing door. "Good morning. Ryne Garages."

"Good morning," a familiar, raspy voice came through the phone line. "My car won't start. I think the battery is dead. I need it towed."

A smile crossed my face. Yep. I knew exactly who that was.

"Are you sure it's the battery, sir?" I asked.

There was a pause. "I know this voice."

I fought a grin.

"Is this Jamie Bell?"

"Sure is, Mr. Daniels."

"Then you know damn well it's my battery, child."

"Did you leave your lights on last night again?"

"It's not me," he replied. "The damn car has a mind of its own. Turns 'em on like magic!"

I'd heard that story before.

I laughed. "I'll see what I can do, Mr. Daniels. I might need a couple of hours."

"I don't have a few hours. I have to see my doctor at two."

"You'll have to ask Steph to pick you up," I said, referring to his six-month pregnant daughter. "I might not be able to get it back to you until tomorrow."

"Tomorrow!" He was aghast. "The service there ain't like it was when your daddy owned it."

"Dad never got your car back to you the same day. He either jump started it or made you wait overnight because he didn't have a chance to get it done."

"Then jump start it."

I pinched the bridge of my nose. "Mr. Daniels, I'll head over to your place with the tow truck and take a look for you, all right?"

He sniffed. "All right. But you get here real soon."

"I'll do my best. See you soon, Mr. Daniels."

"You do that, Jamie." He hung up, and the line buzzed dead.

I put the phone down and slumped against the counter. Mr. Daniels and his forgetfulness where his lights were concerned had long been the bane of my family's existence.

I was an idiot if I thought that wouldn't happen.

"Are you all right?"

"Do you have a tow truck?" I asked Dex.

Well, the question was for him, but I actually asked the diary, where my face was currently planted.

"Of course I have a tow truck," he replied, almost sounding offended that I'd asked such a stupid question. "Why? Did someone crash or something?"

"No." I forced myself to stand up, turn, and look at him. "Mr. Daniels' battery has died, and if I can't jump start it in his drive, I'm gonna need to bring it here."

He blinked at me for a second.

Honestly, his eyelashes were so long it was unfair.

What had I done to not be born with those? Was I a murderer in a previous life?

"I don't know what to deal with first. You thinking you're going to drive my tow truck, or the fact his battery is fucking dead already," Dex said slowly.

"Why the hell shouldn't I drive it?" I said. "And what do you mean already?"

"I sorted that for him about two weeks ago. And you're not driving my truck."

"Two weeks? That's pretty good for him. You know he never turns his lights off, right?" I paused. "And why can't I drive the truck?"

He rubbed his hand over his forehead. "Can we pick one thread of conversation and go with that?"

"Sure." I leaned against the counter and folded my arms. "Why can't I drive your truck?"

"It's new. I don't want anyone to drive it."

"Is it silage season for the farmers, or is that your bullshit I smell?"

He shot me a withering look, even as his lips twitched. "Believe what you want, darlin', but you ain't driving my truck."

I held up my hands. "By all means, you go deal with Mr. Daniels. I've done it for years. I'm happy to pass that task on." I pushed off the counter and headed for the door.

"I didn't say—"

I stood in the doorway and cocked my hip to keep the door open. Raising an eyebrow, I said, "I can't drive the tow truck, and it's a waste of time for me to go if it needs towing. No, you go deal with Mr. Daniels, and I'll sit here and look pretty when you inevitably bring the car in."

His withering look turned a little darker, and his jaw twitched.

He'd talked himself into the most undesirable trip a mechanic in this town could ever make, and he knew it.

Dex: Nil.

Jamie: One.

I licked my finger and swiped a one in thin air. Then, with a wink and a grin, I shut the door and went back into the garage.

Wow.

That cheap point was way more satisfying than it should have been.

---

The loud rumble of the tow truck as it pulled up into the garage's lot.

Clambering over the sofa, I peeked through the blind on the window. A smile crept across my face. It was smug because on the back of the truck was the ancient Ford that Mr. Daniels had been driving for as long as I'd been alive.

It was impressive, to be honest. But there was something to be said for those old cars—especially one that was as well looked after as his was.

"Mr. Daniels," I heard Dex say as he got out. "I told you. It's not your battery, it's your alternator."

"I think you're wrong!" The belligerent old man rounded the truck, finger waving at Dex. "You don't know what you're talking about. The alternator is as good as new."

I snorted. If new was the better part of a decade old, then sure...

"Where's Jamie? I want her to look at it. I don't trust this new blood. Jamie!" He started looking around the lot as if I were hiding in the bushes.

"Mr. Daniels, please go inside to the reception while I unhook your car and bring it into the workshop."

"You'll do nothing of the sort. Jamie will

do that. Jamie! C'mere, child. Stop this damn hooligan manhandling Bettina!"

I let the giggle burst out of me as I jumped off the sofa. Thankfully, the walk through the garage was just long enough that I was able to wipe all traces of amusement from my face. I also grabbed a cloth and wiped my hands as I walked out.

Mr. Daniels didn't miss a thing, and if I didn't look like I'd just been working, he'd call me on my spying.

"Mr. Daniels. Always a pleasure." I sent a playful grin his way. "What's up?"

"What's up?" He waved a wrinkled finger in Dex's direction again.

"Please stop doing that," Dex said wearily. "It's giving me a headache."

Mr. Daniels leaned forward and did it right in his face.

Good God...

Did I leave Dex to his fate, or... No, no. That would be cruel.

Fun, but cruel.

"Okay, okay." I tucked the edge of the dirty cloth into the pocket of my overalls and stepped between them. "Someone explain."

"He says it's my alternator. I don't believe him. He didn't try hard enough on the jumps! I had to cancel my doctor appointment for this mess."

"I tried fifteen times," Dex said. "I looked, and I'm pretty sure it's your alternator. I told you I can't be one hundred percent certain until I can get it into the garage, but you're refusing to let me do it."

"All right. Mr. Daniels, why don't you go take a seat in reception and I'll bring you a nice cup of tea, hmm?" I raised my eyebrows at him.

He glared at me. I'd cut him off before he could respond, clearly.

"While you're enjoying that, I'll help Dex bring in Bettina and take a look. How does that sound?"

"Two sugars," he demanded. "And none of that weak crap your mother tried to serve me once. Let it brew for a minute."

"Yes, sir."

He shuffled off in the direction of the front door.

Dex let out a long breath and slumped against the truck. "Is it always like this here?"

I side-eyed him. "You're a city boy, aren't you?"

"You say that as if it's an insult."

"No insult." I whipped the cloth from my pocket and ran it through my hands. "Just an observation."

"How'd you observe that?" he asked dryly.

I shrugged a shoulder. "Old people in towns like this are set in their ways. You're new—and belligerent old codgers like Edward Daniels won't trust you until he feels like you've proven yourself. He's not trying to be a pain when he wants me to look at it. He just trusts me."

"Really? Because it seems like he's going out of his way to be a pain." He followed me inside.

I tossed the cloth to the side of the sink.

"You're probably not wrong. He is known for being...difficult."

"Difficult." His tone was wry. "You don't say."

I set the tea kettle on the stove top to boil. "Like I said, the old people here are set in their ways. My family have been the only mechanics for eighty-something years. Trusting someone new is hard for them."

"I'll make sure to bring my grandfather and great aunt to the old people center. They'd get on like a house on fire with everyone else."

I laughed and prepared the tea. "You'll get used to it."

"Yeah, all right." He headed for the door. "Next time he calls, I might just let you drive the tow truck."

Ahh, Mr. Daniels and his difficult personality.

Breaking Dexter Ryne down, one dead battery at a time.

———————

Haley stopped, her fry halfway to her mouth. "Seriously? He refused to accept Dex's summary of the situation until he heard you confirm it?"

I nodded.

"Actually, I'm not surprised at all. The old coot was cussing up a storm when the called the office today to cancel his appointment. I could practically feel the steam coming off him down the phone line."

I winced. Between all Dex's grumbles and Mr.

Daniels' louder grumbles, I'd totally forgotten that my best friend was the receptionist at the only surgery clinic in town.

"Ouch. I bet that was fun."

"Oh, it was. I was subjected to ten minutes of complaining about that 'damn little shit in the garage' and I knew for a start he wasn't talking about you."

I paused. "He's not far off in his summary of Dex, to be honest."

"Is he still being a pain in the ass?"

"Still? It's only been one day, Hales. I have another twenty days of his shit. He balked when I said I'd drive the tow truck."

"What is his issue?"

I cupped my boobs, lifted them, then released.

She looked at my chest. "He likes your boobs?"

"I have boobs. You know that."

"Actually, I'm starting to think he's just a dick."

Well, that, too.

I inclined my head in her direction in agreement and picked up my glass of Coke. Sipping through the straw, I cast my gaze away from her and over the rapidly increasing dinner crowd moving into Sherry's Diner.

A staple restaurant in Rivendell, North Carolina, most of the residents here visited it at least once a week. Breakfast, lunch, dinner—it didn't matter. Sherry's was the place to go for gossip or news and everything else in between.

I just came for the burgers.

A low whistle left Haley's parted lips. "Who is that?"

I swung my head around, glancing at her to see where she was looking so I could follow her line of sight. She was looking at the door.

At the guy who was standing in it, looking around at the people who filled the recently-refurbished diner.

"Oh no." The groan escaped me before I could stop it. "I have to hide."

Haley blinked at me, then looked back at Dex. "Oh, shit. Is that—?"

"Dex? Yep."

She tilted her head to the side. "He doesn't look like a mechanic."

"Is there a way we're supposed to look?"

"I expected him to be dirty. You know. Oily and shit."

I just barely resisted rolling my eyes. "He was when I left two hours ago."

Haley jolted her head, facing me with her eyes wide. "I think he saw you. He's coming this way."

I glanced over my shoulder. Shit. She was right. "Thanks. He probably felt your beady little eyes undressing him."

She shrugged a shoulder with a half-grin on her face. "As long as he keeps his mouth shut..."

I kicked her under the table seconds before a shadow fell over it and us. "Are you following me?" I asked, turning to face him.

Dex laughed and held up his hands. "Sure. I've been following you for the past two hours, yet somehow managed to go home, shower, and get a take-out order for my entire family."

"I wouldn't put it past you."

"I'll keep that in mind." His eyes twinkled, then he turned his attention to Haley. "We haven't met. Dex Ryne."

Haley took his outstretched hand, a girlish smile lighting up her face.

Sweet baby Jesus in a chicken coop.

"Haley Allen. A pleasure."

Barf.

"It's all mine."

Double barf.

"I'm about to order food. Can I get you ladies anything?" He glanced between us.

"We're good," I said tightly. "Thank you."

Dex's lips twitched, and he raised a hand as he headed to join the line.

Haley stared after him.

I snapped my fingers in front of her face. "Earth to Haley."

"Man, that's a great ass," she said lazily, turning back to face him. "Have you seen that ass?"

Of course, I jerked my head around and got an eyeful of the way his bleach-wash jeans hugged what was, obviously, a very peachy backside.

"Oh, for God's sake," I muttered, focusing back on her and jabbing a fry in my ketchup. "Why were you so nice to him?"

"He's pretty," she replied with a straight face. "Like I said... As long as he doesn't talk..."

I rolled my eyes. "I need the bathroom before I vomit on my dinner."

I got up, leaving her laughing to herself at the table.

# 6

## DEX

I smirked when I glanced over and saw Jamie throwing a napkin on the table. She slid out of her booth, her shorts riding up her thighs and almost giving a peek at the curve of her ass cheeks as she straightened up.

She stormed off, leaving Haley laughing, and disappeared around the corner.

I looked away before Haley caught my eye. The last thing I wanted was her to think I was trying to get her attention when I'd just been eying up Jamie's ass.

Not that I had a place doing so, but still. With an ass like that...

I shook my head to rid my mind of those thoughts. She might have a great ass, but she was a big fucking pain in mine. Her stupid, smart mouth. Her ridiculous, sassy comments. That fucking pretty smile she got when she knew she had me.

The one she'd given me after the tow truck

conversation this morning when I realized I'd talked myself into the worst job I'd do this week.

That was fucking stupid. And all it'd made me do was realize that she was cute as fuck when she smiled like that—especially when she had a grease smudge over her cheek.

The craziest part was that her lipstick had still been intact at the end of the day. That'd been some goddamn sorcery right there.

The person in front of me in line stepped aside, so I moved forward and placed my order.

"That's a twenty-minute wait. Is that okay?" The pretty, young redhead asked me, blinking bright blue eyes in my direction.

I waved my hand. "Fine. I'll go take a seat with some friends."

She nodded. "Cash or card?"

I pulled my card out of my pocket and swiped when she motioned to.

"Here's your number." She handed me a receipt with the number circled on the top. "The machine will call out when your order is ready, and you can collect it from the other end of the counter." She pointed to an area with a "Take-Out Collection" sign hanging above it.

"You got it. Thanks." I stuffed my card back in my pocket and folded the receipt in two. A glance at where Haley was sitting told me Jamie hadn't returned from wherever she'd disappeared to.

Going up there, to that table, was a bad idea. After all, one of the women took pleasure in pissing me off and the other obviously was mildly interested in just the pleasure.

Which is why I went up there. Because I was fucking good at bad ideas.

Case in point: I'd hired the woman who took pleasure in pissing me off.

"Do you mind?" I motioned to the empty side of the booth where Jamie had been sitting.

Haley looked up, straw between her bright-pink lips. "I don't," she said. "But Jamie probably will."

"Perfect." I slid across the booth, gently pushing her plate toward the edge of the table.

Haley's lips curved. "I take it you haven't been introduced to her temper yet."

"It can't be worse than her sarcasm."

She laughed, but it was almost hollow. "Boy, you're brave. You're playing with fire."

I grinned. "I turned my grandfather gray with all the ones I used to set as a kid. I think I can handle Jamie Bell."

Her eyebrows shot up. "Brave *and* stupid. I give you a week before she chews you up and spits you out on the sidewalk."

"You don't know me."

"And you don't know her, yet you seem to assume you can handle her."

"Her and her hot temper, right?" She had a bad attitude—not a hot temper. They were wildly different.

Haley leaned back in the booth and studied me. "You know, she told me you were a dick, and now I see it. You're not so pretty anymore."

I fought a laugh. "Pretty? That's the first time I've ever been called pretty by someone that wasn't my niece."

"Kids. Always there for an ego boost. My nephew is the same." She folded her arms.

"This is cozy," Jamie said, approaching the table. "Sure, take my seat, Dex. Would you like to finish my burger, too?"

"Nah, I'm good. I have my own cooking." I nodded toward the counter. "Feel free to sit next to me."

She motioned to Haley to move up. Haley rolled her eyes, but she slid over so Jamie could sit next to her. "What are you doing here?"

"Your politeness is astounding," I replied.

She hit me with a flat stare.

"Waiting for food," I continued. "I asked, and Haley said she didn't mind."

"I mind."

"That's what I said," Haley muttered.

Jamie shot her a look, then at me. "Isn't it bad enough I have to spend nine hours a day in a garage with you? Now, I have to ruin my dinner, too?"

I leaned back and rested my arm across the top of the booth seat. "It's your choice to be in the garage, darlin'. You can leave any time."

"And pass the chance to beat the sexism out of you?" She raised an eyebrow. "I'll take my chances at passing out from stress, thanks."

A robotic voice called out my number.

"You should try being nice." My lips twitched

as I moved across the leather seat. "You never know. You might find that you like me." I winked at Haley. "See you soon."

Jamie didn't reply, but her gaze followed me as I grabbed my food order and then snaked my way through the diner.

I stopped at the door and caught her eye.

She held my gaze for all of a second before she turned away.

I had no idea what to make of her.

---

My sister's piercing blue gaze followed me around the garage. "Please, Dex. It's just for an hour."

"Rox," I said softly. "I cannot have Charley running around the garage when I'm working."

"One hour," she begged, tucking her dark curls behind her ear. "Please. This interview is important to me."

"What about Grandpa? Or Greta?"

Roxy groaned and leaned against the wall. "Greta terrifies her, you know that."

"She terrifies me, and I'm twenty-eight," I muttered.

"Exactly! Come on. Look at her. She's sitting in there not making a sound." She waved a red-tipped finger toward the staff room where Charley, my seven-year-old niece was sitting as quiet as a mouse, coloring in some genie pictures from her most recent obsession. "She won't bug you. If I get this job, you won't have to look after her anymore during the day in the school breaks. Please?"

I rubbed my hand down my face. "You didn't tell me why Grandpa can't have her."

"The last time, he fell asleep. She tried her hand and baking and almost set the kitchen on fire," she told me slowly.

"That was two fu—years ago," I corrected myself halfway through. "Come on, Rox. You know this isn't practical. I have my new employee I have to keep an eye on and I can't do both."

Her dark eyebrows shot up. "Why? Because you keep arguing with her? No—don't you dare argue with me, Dexter. Grandpa told me how thrilled you were to hire her."

"She's a woman!"

My sister planted her hands on her hips and hit me with a stare that would take down Floyd Mayweather.

"And what," she began very slowly, in a terrifyingly low voice, "is that supposed to mean?"

I coughed, rubbing the back of my neck, and took a step back. I half-tripped on a wrench but managed to right myself. "Nothing. Just that this," I waved my arms, "maybe isn't the right place for her."

"Oh boy." She dropped the threatening tone and moved straight to sarcasm. "I'm so thrilled my daughter has such a positive, uplifting male influence in her life."

"Hey." I pointed at her. "Charley can be whatever she wants to be."

"As long as it isn't in your garage."

"As long as it isn't in my garage," I repeated with a nod of my head. "My garage, my rules."

"Technically," she pointed out. "It's Grandpa's garage. You just run it."

"Don't weigh this conversation down with semantics, Rox. You'll never see that I'm right and you're wrong if you do that."

"Oh, good," Jamie's voice came from the side door. "It's good to know I'm not the only woman he's insufferable toward."

My sister's lips curved into a cunning smile, and her eyes glinted with mischief.

Shit, no.

Fucking hell.

I knew that look.

Roxy turned on the balls of her feet and looked at Jamie. "You must be Jamie, the poor soul who has to work for the demon that is my baby brother."

"Oh, Jesus. Here we go," I moaned, wiping my hand down my face.

Jamie nodded solemnly. "That's me."

"Roxy." My sister held a hand out to Jamie, and they shook. Then, she tossed her hair over her shoulder and met my eyes. "So, you'll watch Charley for an hour? Thanks, Dex. I appreciate it."

"Wait, no—damn it, Roxanne!" I scooted past Jamie and chased after her. "Rox!"

"What?" My sister asked with a long-suffering sigh as she turned right in front of her car.

"You can't leave Charley here," I said. "I cannot have her here while I'm working."

She held up her hands, her key dangling from her middle finger. "I have nobody else to have her, you know that. And I need this interview. I told you. One hour." She unlocked her car and opened the door. "Besides. You'll have to be nice to Jamie in front of her."

Bitch.

"I'm not the one with the attitude problem. And you have sixty minutes, Rox. If you're late, you owe me big time."

"Yeah, yeah. Whatever." She got in her car and started it.

I stared after her as she left. Shaking my head, I took a deep breath and went back inside.

"Uncle Dex?" Charley said from the doorway.

"Yep?" I turned to her.

She folded her arms across her chest. "Mom only did that so you have to be nice to her." With one finger, she pointed at Jamie.

"She mentioned it," I said tightly.

"And she could have left me at home with Pops because I don't bake cakes on my own anymore."

"We all learned a lesson that day."

"She didn't even ask Pops," Charley went on, innocence crossing all of her features. "She told him she had a babysitter and we came here."

Jamie snorted from behind me. I shot her a dark look.

"Good to know, Char, thanks. Anything else your mom didn't want to tell me?"

She thought for a moment, her light brown eyebrows drawing together in a frown. "Oh, yes!" She brightened, then dropped the smile.

"Well?"

She looked around as if she knew what she was saying was bad. "She said you're a word that I'm not allowed to say until I can touch the ceiling without my tippy-toes."

Jamie did more than snort at that. She laughed.

I didn't.

"All right. That's enough of that for today. Why don't you go finish your coloring?"

"Will you hang it on the wall here?"

"I'll hang ten pictures if you color them nicely and let me get back to work."

She grinned. It was almost a manic one— one that told me I'd just made a huge mistake. "Okay!" She skipped back into the staff room and jumped on the sofa.

I watched as she got comfortable in front of her coloring things.

"Well, if your sister thinks you're a word a kid can't repeat, I can't be far wrong in my estimation of you." Jamie flashed me a grin as she walked past me.

"Good morning. How are you? Did you sleep well?" I tried to keep the sarcasm out of my tone, but I don't think it worked.

"Good morning." She kept the same, bright tone. "I'm excellent, and I slept exceptionally."

"I'm so glad."

"I dreamed I beat a mechanic over the head with numerous tools," she continued. "It was delightful, and I woke in a great mood."

I stared at the back of her head as she rifled inside a toolbox.

"Ah-ha," she said, pulling something out. She turned, then froze. "Why are you looking at me like that?"

"I'm trying to be nice," I said through gritted teeth. "But it's hard when you're informing me you dreamed of murdering me."

"You asked how I slept."

"Not what you dreamed about."

She held her hands up. "Well, I'm in a great mood, and I'd like to stay that way."

I blinked at her. "I'm scared of you in a good mood."

"You should be." She waggled her eyebrows once as if she were warning me, then slipped past me.

I watched her go. "There are so many things I'd like to say to you right now."

"Which are?"

"For a start, why aren't you wearing overalls?"

"It's hot," she replied.

"So put them on and drink a bit more water."

She put the screwdriver down on the side and planted a hand on the hood of the Honda she was about to work on. "Now, you're just being awkward because you have to keep your sarcasm in check."

"It's not sarcasm when I'm talking to you." I

took the tool from her hand and replaced it with the correct size. "It's survival skills."

She switched the screwdrivers right back out. "Fifty bucks says you're dead before lunch, then."

I threw the screwdriver back in the toolbox. "We're going to continue this later when I don't have to hold back."

"I can't wait." She grinned and, reaching inside the car, popped the hood.

"I need a coffee," I muttered.

"Ooh, that'd be great. Cream and two sugars, please."

"I wasn't offering."

"I know. I wasn't asking."

"Give me some goddamn strength," I muttered again, walking away to the tune of her muffled laughter.

I stormed past the sofa where Charley was coloring some tiny tiger in blue and hit the power button for the coffee machine.

"I like her."

I turned around. Charley hadn't even looked up from her coloring. "Huh?" I said.

"Jamie," she said, absentmindedly tucking a loose curl away from her face. She peered up. "I like her."

"Of course you do," I replied.

"She doesn't take any of your banana-split."

I frowned. "My banana-split?"

"Yeah. I have to call it banana-split."

"I don't know what that is."

She paused. "Will you tell mom if I say a bad

word?"

I drew a cross over my heart in promise.

"Bullshit," she whispered. "Banana-split."

I grimaced.

Bullshit. Banana-split.

Awesome. Now my sister was teaching my niece how to politely call me on it.

"Gotcha."

"See? She doesn't take your banana-split. I like that in a woman."

"Charley, you have got to stop listening to your mom."

"Why would I do that? If I stop listening, I won't know how to tattle on her to you."

I pointed a finger at her. "Good point. Here." I dug in my pocket and pulled out a five-dollar bill. "For your troubles." I tossed it on top of her coloring.

She picked it up and stuffed it in her bag. "Gotta start charging more," she murmured.

Yep. The kid was a Ryne all right.

# 7

## JAMIE

"Three hours," Dex said flatly, handing Roxy a pink backpack. "Three hours."

"I'm sorry." She pressed her hands to her chest. "The interview went on a little longer than I thought, then a friend invited me to lunch. I knew she wouldn't be a problem."

Dex dug in his pocket and pulled out his cell phone. "See this? It's called a phone. It has this really neat feature where you can call people and talk to them to tell them things. Like if you're going to be two hours late."

Charley rolled her eyes. "Mom never uses her phone."

"I never use my phone to speak to your uncle," Roxy corrected her.

"I know. I called you twenty times."

"Thirty-three," she replied. "My phone was on silent."

"You're such a banana-splitter," he snapped.

Roxy grinned, clearly holding back a laugh. "How's it feel to look in the mirror?"

"Get out of my garage." He waved his hand at her. "And tell Aunt Greta to make sure she has a bra on when I get home. She scarred me for life this morning."

I covered my mouth with my hand to hide my laughter.

Roxy caught my eye and smiled, her tongue caught between her teeth. She wiggled her fingers right before she ushered Charley out of the garage and across to her car.

"Women. You're all out to get me."

"Have you considered you're the common denominator here?" I asked, leaning against the side of the car I'd been working on all morning. "Me, your sister, your niece..."

He sighed at me. "I'm too tired to fight you."

"What's with the banana-split thing?"

Another hand wave. "Apparently, Charley picked up on Roxy calling me on my bullshit one too many times, so Charley now calls bullshit, banana-split. And uses it to call me on it."

I laughed. "That's the most random thing I've ever heard."

"Well, I discovered it when Charley told me she liked you after five minutes because you don't take my banana-split."

"She's gonna go so far in life," I mused. "And she's right. I don't."

"Much to my annoyance."

"Really? It annoys you that I fight you on

everything? Oh my God. It's not obvious at all."

He turned to look at me. "I can't decide if sarcasm is your default setting, or you're deliberately trying to wind me up to the point I fire you."

"That would shorten this torturous three weeks into something a little less...long."

His lips twitched to the side. "I'm not going to fire you, Jamie. No matter how much you get under my skin. It'd be much more enjoyable to see you break first."

I raised an eyebrow. "I'm sorry to disappoint you. I don't break. I might bend a little, but I don't break. If you think the fact I can't stand to be in your presence means I'm going to throw in the towel, you need to have a rethink. If anyone breaks here, it'll be you."

He took a step closer to me, amusement still shining in his eyes. "I love your arrogance. I can't wait to see you realize you're in over your head with me."

I pushed off the car, annoyance pulsing through my veins. One step, two steps—I was right in front of him, almost nose-to-nose. And I was rapidly giving in to my anger.

"My arrogance?" I asked in a low voice. "Are you familiar with your own?"

"I prefer confidence." He smirked, something sparking in his bright blue eyes. "For me, that is. Arrogance definitely fits you better."

He went to move away, but I wasn't done.

"I grew up in this garage."

He froze.

I pinned him with my gaze. "Whoever owns this garage bought it from my father. So, since you think I can't hack it, you should know that I was a girl in a man's world before I was ever a woman in a man's world."

He held my gaze. Unwaveringly. The harshness with which he stared at me sent a shiver down my spine, but I fought it.

I wouldn't give him the satisfaction of knowing he'd affected me.

Without breaking eye contact, he tilted his head to the side, just a tiny bit. Then, he lifted one grease-coated, roughened hand to the side of my face, and using two fingertips, pushed some of my thick, unruly hair behind my ear.

I swallowed when he lowered his mouth to the side of my face, lips almost ghosting over my skin until a breath of air separated his mouth and my ear.

"That might be right," he said in a low, rough voice. "But you've never been in my world, Jamie. It's not a man's world I don't think you can hack— it's mine."

He released my hair and pulled back from me.

Goosebumps prickled across my skin. The further away from me he walked, the more I was aware of the chill that wafted across my skin courtesy of the air-con.

I took a deep breath.

For a moment, it was as if he'd stolen the oxygen from around me and blocked out the cold breeze.

For a moment, I'd almost wanted his lips to brush my skin.

And on that note, I knew I had to leave for lunch.

---

I blinked at my clock. My heart was racing a thousand miles an hour, and even as I stared at the red, LED number on the screen, I couldn't make it out.

I gave up, instead rolling over and running my hand through the matted mess that was my hair. I could feel the sweat sticking to my body, and my feet were so tangled in the sheets I knew I'd have to change them before I left this morning.

I peered over my shoulder at the cloth once I'd gotten my breathing under control.

Five-fifteen a.m. Over an hour before my alarm, and I was awake for one simple reason.

The kiss in that dream had been all too real.

The faceless, nameless person that Sleep Jamie had been playing tonsil tennis with was identifiable by one fact only.

He smelt like coffee and motor oil.

Not a particularly desirable scent, but one that, to me, weirdly, was attractive.

I only knew one person who smelt like that, and his name was Dexter Ryne.

I wasn't surprised. After our...moment... yesterday, neither of us had said a word to the other. God knows why he didn't speak, but I was silent because I had a startling realization over lunch.

I was attracted to him.

Pin me down, flip me over, fuck me 'til next week attracted to him.

I'd almost dropped my damn sandwich.

I wasn't okay with this. He was handsome, sure, but he was also an asshole. I could say that with absolute confidence, because I, too, was an asshole.

Takes one to know one, after all.

But it was the way he'd come up to me. I'd relived it a hundred times, and I felt like a goddamn schoolgirl by the time I'd gone to bed last night.

Something which had apparently let my subconscious slut out to play.

Obviously, I'd deprived her of sexy dreams for a while.

No.

Dex.

Goddamn it.

The way he'd held his ground, kept eye contact, smoothed my hair with his rough hand. The gentle way he'd drawn me in until he'd whispered in my ear.

Whispered something that sounded a lot like both a threat and a promise.

A threat that I couldn't hack it, and the promise that he'd prove it.

But what was his world?

Was he going to throw jobs at me he didn't think I could do, or was he going to use another weapon—himself?

Because I could do all the first. There wasn't a thing I couldn't fix.

He was another matter.

I wasn't weak. I had no doubt I'd be able to resist him, but I was also human. If I was attracted to him, I'd give in eventually. He wouldn't win the battle of the mechanics, but he might just win the battle of seduction.

If he wanted to go that way.

Hell, maybe he wasn't even attracted to me. Maybe he was just a touchy, flirty asshole who got off on making women feel like he wanted him. If that was true, then fine. That would make it easier if he wanted to pretend to want me.

I talked a good game.

That was my only thought as I scrambled out of the sweaty sheets. I tugged them all off and threw them into a ball beneath my window, then trudged into the shower.

If I was going to think deep thoughts, I might as well get clean at the same time.

I stripped off and threw my clothes in the laundry hamper, then started the shower. It was way too cold when I got in, but I was too tired to care. It heated up quickly enough, and once the chill had left my skin, my mind wandered back to my previous train of thought.

Dex.

What was I thinking? I didn't like him, and

just two days ago, I'd been disgusted that Haley obviously wanted to jump his bones.

Now, I kinda wanted to.

More to the point, I kinda wanted to know if Real Dex kissed better than Dream Dex. And that was a high bar to beat...

I smacked myself on the forehead. What was wrong with me? What the hell was I doing, standing in the shower lamenting a dream? There were thousands of mechanics in this country who probably smelt like coffee and motor oil.

Maybe I'd kissed one of them. They didn't have faces as far as I was concerned, after all.

Yeah, I'd kissed one of those. Not Dex. Not the asshole boss who flicked my sarcasm switch before I'd even parked my car outside the garage. Not the dickhead guy who thought I couldn't handle the job and underestimated me at every turn.

No, no, no. I'd most definitely not dreamed about kissing him and lifting up his shirt to run my fingers over his...

I needed therapy. Clearly, that was the only option presented to me at this time.

Or...alcohol and carbs would work. They were cheaper than therapy...

---

"Or quitting!" Haley snapped at me from the treadmill next to me once I was done weighing up therapy or carbs. "He doesn't respect you, Jamie.

He doesn't believe you're good enough. He thinks he can handle your temper, for the love of God. You can't even handle your temper!"

"Your date went well last night, then," I replied dryly, grabbing my water bottle.

"No. It was a hot freakin' mess because daddy's boy was thirty minutes late and accused me of being rude when I wanted to leave."

"You ordered the lobster, didn't you?"

"Damn fucking right I ordered the lobster," she continued. "But we're not talking about me, we're talking about you and your idiocy."

"Can I remind you this job is still your fault?"

"No, you can't. Because, if you do, I lose the moral high ground, and I look good sitting up here."

"This job is still your fault."

"Motherfuh." She jabbed the button to slow it down since she was huffing in earnest now.

Anger? Exhaustion? Who could tell? Flip a coin and you'd still never know.

She sucked at the bottle with the vigor of a two-dollar hooker until she'd calmed down. Towel in hand, she wiped her face. "Look, I was all for it until I met the guy."

I was sensing a theme here...

"He's an ass, James. And now you're attracted to him?"

I refrained from pointing out she was like a panting puppy with a dog treat when she first laid eyes on him.

"And yes, I appreciate I was a little googly-eyed when I met him," she added, one finger lifted in my direction. "But this is not good. You cannot be attracted to someone who undervalues you that much."

"I know tha—"

"He's a self-righteous little prick who needs to be taught a lesson."

"That's wha—"

"How do you work with him? Just thinking about him is making me angry."

"Can I speak now?" I forced out, getting off the treadmill.

She blinked at me. "Sure. Sorry. I got carried away."

No shit, Sherlock.

"I know he undervalues me. I know he's a self-righteous little prick. But I'm not saying I'm going to bonk his brains out for the next six months." I pushed the door to the hall open and let her pass. "I was actually asking your advice on how to deal with working with him and being attracted to him before you went off on your tirade."

"Oh."

"Yes, oh."

"Well, this is awkward." Haley pushed open the door to the dressing room and held it for me. I thanked her and passed. "I don't know if I'm honest. I would say just avoid any situations where it might get a little bit heated—"

"So, don't speak to him at all."

She paused. "Mm, yeah. That was a bit of a turn on the other night at dinner. Is that how you'd foreplay?"

"Haley. Not helping."

"Sure, sure." We grabbed our bags from the lockers and headed for the showers. "But still, watch out for that."

"Thanks. Observant of you."

She grinned. "Just remember that no matter how hot he is or how tingly he makes your lady bits, he's a sexist asshole who doesn't have the capacity to give you the respect a badass chick such as yourself deserves."

I paused outside my shower room. "Wow. They should hire you to give motivational speeches to college students."

She glared at me. "Go fuck yourself," she said, then slammed the door.

"Not a bad idea!"

# 8

## DEX

I kicked the fridge shut and glanced at the clock. I had one hour of peace left before the red-lipped pain in my ass showed up to start work, and I was going to relish every second of it.

Mostly because it was seconds where I wasn't thinking about what she'd taste like if I kissed her.

I hadn't meant to get so close to her yesterday. In fact, I didn't want to be anywhere near her, but when she'd stood up against me and dropped the bombshell that this was the garage her family used to own, I couldn't stop.

She'd been too close.

Too tempting.

I could have walked away, but she had a terrible habit of making some of the things she said sound like a challenge. If there was one thing I couldn't walk away from, it was a challenge.

The biggest problem?

*Jamie was a challenge.*

A loud-mouthed, confident, damn tempting challenge who didn't wear pants unless they were sassy.

I wanted to see it—see her—through. Figure it out. Figure her out. Figure out why she was so damn headstrong and confident and determined to prove me wrong.

Nothing could or would make me believe she needed to be in my garage. Nothing would make me change my mind on that.

She was a liability. It was harsh, but it was the way I felt. And as long as I was in control of hiring in this place, that's the way it would be.

Maybe that made me an asshole.

I never pretended I wasn't one.

I stirred the sugar into my coffee. The spoon clinked against the countertop when I dropped it down, and I picked up the steaming hot mug.

My foot tapped against the floor.

How the fuck was I going to get through the next three weeks? She'd worked for me for all of two days, and already, I was thinking about all the ways I wanted to flip her over and fuck her senseless.

I was attracted to her beyond belief. There wasn't a time I glanced over at her working that her red lips or blue eyes didn't make me think things I had no place thinking.

Like how she'd look with her lips around my cock and those eyes looking up at me.

How her ass would look if she were bent over the hood of that Mustang she drove, with my fingers digging into her ass cheeks.

How she'd look if my face was between her legs and she was halfway through coming all over my tongue.

I reached down and adjusted my jeans. My cock was hardening at the thoughts that were running through my head. That was something I had to get under control.

Not that my cock had ever fucking listened to me.

I'd tried to make it listen, but it never did.

Damn thing had a mind of its own.

I rubbed my hand down my face. Fucking hell. I was slowly getting obsessed with the woman I worked with, and she was everything I hated.

She was mouthy. Determined. Strong. Confident. Unafraid to challenge me. Unhesitant to call me on the bullshit I spewed every now and then. She was a force of nature—the human equivalent of a hurricane that ripped through a state viciously.

Except I had no doubt she had the ability to rip through a person, too.

I sipped the coffee.

I had to rethink this. Had to get these thoughts the fuck out of my head. There was nothing good about any of this.

Fucking hell.

I'd said fuck more times in the last forty-eight hours than I had in my entire life.

Fuck, fuck, fuck, fuck, fuck.

That wasn't helping, given that was what I

wanted to do to her.

I put my cup on the coffee table and threw myself on the sofa. Springs creaked beneath my weight, but I ignored them as I got comfy and pulled the cup onto my lap.

It burned my skin under my jeans.

Fucking machine.

I rested the mug on the arm of the sofa and stared out of the window where she'd park that Mustang of hers. It matched the color of her eyes to perfection.

Was that its original color or coincidence?

Shit, why the fuck did I care?

All I should be caring about was replacing the fuel injector in my grandpa's Dodge Ram. The fuel injector that was delayed from the supplier and sending him ten shades of fucking insane.

That reminded me. I needed to call them right about now.

I took a huge gulp of my coffee and grabbed the phone.

---

"Motherfucker!" Jamie's voice echoed across the garage.

I straightened and looked toward the door. "Hi."

"Don't you 'hi' me," she snapped, kicking something that looked a lot like a screwdriver across the floor.

It skidded and landed a few feet from me.

Yep, screwdriver.

"Hello?" I offered. "Howdy? How'd you do? How are you? Bonjour? Ciao? Hola?"

She nailed me with a stare that would make granite soften. "Hey," she replied. "Do you usually leave your tools on the floor?"

I gazed around at the tool-strewn floor of the garage. "Do you not look where you're walking?"

"That's it!" Bending down, she retrieved a tiny wrench from the floor. "I'm getting this cesspit under control!" Turning, she threw it at a box, only for it to bounce off the metal surface and back onto the floor.

The clang echoed through the garage.

"My God!" she shouted.

Except, it was more like a screech than anything.

"How do you work like this? There are tools everywhere. Do you believe you can run a reputable garage when the only thing you can find without looking is the coffee machine?"

I opened my mouth to reply.

It didn't matter.

"Your wrenches are all over the place. Your screwdrivers arc so screwed you've basically fed them to hookers. Your toolboxes are so unorganized you make teenage boys look tidy. And don't get me sorted on your paperwork!" She jabbed a blood-red nail my way. "Did you fix Senator Yale's car last week or last year? Was Mayor Reynolds' truck last month or in January? Did you take tow Alistair Walter's bus on August fifth or April fifth?"

I opened my mouth once again.

"My God!" she carried on yet again. "This is not how you run a business, Dexter Ryne! I don't care if you pay your taxes. I don't care if you pay me on time. This isn't a freaking big city. You keep your customers in order and you make them feel like they're all you have. Do you understand that?"

Another open-mouthed attempt was all I shot her way.

"You tell Senator Yale you remember his previous issues and you need to check it over even if you've forgotten. You tell Mr. Daniels that you can charge his battery." She prodded her finger at me. "You—"

"Shut up," I said wearily.

Jamie bristled. "What?"

"Shit up," I repeated.

She stared at me.

"Unless you're going to tell me something about this godforsaken town I don't know, shut the fuck up," I continued. "I don't know what the hell wormed its way up your ass this morning, but you have thirty minutes to make sure it wriggles its way out of your asshole."

She stared at me.

"And while you're getting rid of that worm infestation...Tidy those wrenches, would ya, darlin'?"

"Oh my God!" she shouted as I shut the staff room door behind me.

Hey.
Life was a minefield.
And she was a whole damn battlefield.

# 9

## JAMIE

"Spineless, selfish little prick."

I slammed four wrenches into the box. "Weak little dickhead."

I snatched up three crosshead screwdrivers, yanked open a drawer, and threw them against the metal base.

It closed with a satisfying clang.

"Arrogant little pencil dick." I tugged open the top drawer and dropped a handful of nuts into it.

Not the decent kind of nuts, either.

Clang, clink, clang, clink.

They rattled across the tiny drawer like a miniature, angry army. I pushed the drawer shut with some crazy vigor.

I was angry from my dream.

That was insane. It was completely fucking crazy that I was so angry from something my subconscious mind had dreamed up, yet here I was.

Alongside Dex. Wearing nothing but light-blue jeans with numerous stains and a light grey tank top that showed off all his muscles. If he'd set a rule about overalls, he hadn't made it universal, clearly.

Thank God I was wearing nothing but a spaghetti-strap shirt and a pair of workout shorts.

What was good for the goose was good for the gander, my grandma had always taught me.

But she'd lived thirty years in England, so who the hell knew what she really meant by that?

I slammed a drawer shut. It clanged through the garage, clanging off the stone walls.

I didn't even know what I was insulting. I think it was thin air at this point. There was something satisfying about shouting into thin air, though.

I glanced over my shoulder. Dex was bent over at the waist, fitting Mr. Daniels' alternator. His light-blue jeans were low-slung and did nothing for the base desire I was currently battling. His shirt had ridden up, and as I peered across the garage, I could see the dimples that decorated the base of his lower back. The muscles that hinted at more to come.

The deeper the muscle, the lower it dipped, right?

Right.

Wrong, Jamie. Wrong, Jamie. That was not how we did this right now.

I shook off those thoughts and dragged my attention away. I was going to hurt myself if I carried on thinking these thoughts.

"It's been five minutes since you insulted a tool." Dex's voice rumbled across the garage. "You all right, darlin'?"

"It's been five minutes since I stopped killing you in my mind." The words escaped me right as I twisted the cap on the oil tank and pulled out the dipstick. Too low. I tapped the end of the stick against the side of the twisting cap and set it to the side.

"Is that a record?"

I put a funnel in the hole and studied the height of the oil. "Must be," I replied, dropping the stick. I crossed the garage and pulled the correct oil from the shelf.

"You sure that's the right one?" Dex asked.

"Want me to pour it over you and throw a match to be sure?" I unscrewed the cap and slowly poured it into the funnel until the tank was full.

"I'm good. Double-checking is your friend, Jamie."

I capped the bottle and re-shelved it. "Mhmm." I screwed the cap back onto the oil tank and moved to the engine oil. The level read fine, but I topped it up a couple inches to be safe. Same with the brake fluid.

This was a standard service. Doubting me was such an insult.

Most non-mechanics knew how to do this, for the love of God.

Even Haley could top up her goddamn brake fluid. Why she couldn't do the oil was nobody's business.

I screwed the cap for the brake fluid back on so tight there was no chance Mr. Elvin's grandson would try to top it up again—six months ago, he'd mistaken that for engine oil.

That had been a costly mistake for my dad... and for Mr. Elvin.

Mostly for Mr. Elvin, granted, but still.

I grabbed the sheets that detailed what other work needed doing on the car. It was only the windscreen wipers, so I crossed out what I'd just done and set the sheets down on the toolbox next to me. I unhooked the hood and pushed it back down into place.

"Done?" Dex asked.

I shook my head. "Have to change the wiper blades."

"Back-ordered," he replied, straightening up and only just avoiding banging his head. "Gonna be another two days."

I blinked at him. "Why'd you book it if you don't have them?"

What kind of garage was out of stock of wiper blades?

He came over and picked up the sheet. His blue eyes scanned it side to side before he shook his head and handed me the sheet. "I booked it two weeks ago. They're back-ordered at the supplier. There's nothing I can do."

"I told him he'd have it today." I slumped back against it. "Ugh. This is annoying."

"Call him." Dex grabbed a bottle of water from the floor and unscrewed it. "Tell him we'll call him as soon as they're in stock and make sure they're fitted the moment he walks through the door."

"No, no. You can call him." I shook my head so vehemently I felt dizzy. "He makes Mr. Daniels look like a puppy."

Dex faltered for a moment, his cheeks puffing out as he held the water in his mouth. He stared at me for a second before he swallowed and re-capped the bottle. "Well, maybe we should try to find some wipers today."

"You think?"

"Don't get snarky. How did I know I was moving to a town full of year-long Scrooges?"

"They're not Scrooges. They're..." I hesitated. A word didn't spring to mind.

"Set in their ways," I know, he said wryly. "You've said. Right. Where would we stand a chance at getting some wiper blades from today?"

I twisted my lips to the side. "Well, there's the auto place the next town over. They usually have plenty in stock. And there's a great taco place next door. I'll get lunch at the same time."

"Whoa, wait. Why do you get to go?"

"Do you know the auto place I'm talking about?"

Dex clicked his tongue. "No, but I heard something about a great taco place, so..."

"And?"

"And it seems like I should know where this great taco place—I mean, the auto place—is. You should take me."

"I'm not taking you for lunch. I'd rather eat in

a dumpster."

"You're so charming. By the way, Jamie, are you single?"

I flipped him the bird. "Fine. I can see I'm not going to get out of this, and I need wipers, so fine. You win. But you're buying your own tacos, and I'm driving."

He pulled his keys out of his pocket. "I'm driving. You can direct me."

"No." I folded my arms across my chest. "In my experience, there's one thing men cannot do and that is listen to directions."

"Well, if that's all you think I can't do." He flashed me a wolfish grin and grabbed his phone from the counter to his left. "Come on, Jamie. Show me this great taco place."

"And buy the wiper blades. I hope you've got your credit card, Dex."

He patted his pocket. "Right there. Let's go."

---

"I told you to go left."

"I went left!"

"No, you went left two junctions too late."

"They were close together!" Dex smacked the steering wheel. "Now where do we go?"

"If you'd be quiet, I can try and find out." I loaded Google Maps on my phone.

"You're the one bitching."

"If you'd taken the right junction, I wouldn't have to bitch. Why don't you have a GPS in this monster?" Seriously, his truck was huge and basically brand new—and there was no GPS.

It was like twenty-fifteen and the nineteen-eighties had a baby.

"Because it was a pointless extra expense given that I don't listen to instructions," he drawled, tapping his fingers against the steering wheel. "You're the one who was born here. Don't you know where we are?"

"If I did, we wouldn't be lost," I ground out through my clamped jaw. "Thank God." The little blue line popped up on my screen. "Right."

"Go right?" Dex turned the key.

"No, I mean "right" as in, right, let's go."

"If you use it like that again and I go right, it's on you."

"Dex, shut up and drive."

He shot me a look, but he did as I said.

"Go slow," I instructed. "In case you miss a turn again."

"It was hidden!"

I rolled my eyes. "Five minutes ago, they were too close together. Keep your banana split straight, would you?"

He caught my eye. His lips twitched. "Where am I going now?"

"Keep going." I didn't want to think about the way a tiny shiver danced over the back of my neck at the tiny smile that played over his lips. "And take the first right."

"Got it." Luckily for me, he took it correctly.

Somehow, we made it out from the middle

of nowhere to the main road, and I was able to direct him. He drove a little slower—the kind of slow that makes you cuss out other drivers when you're behind them—but hey, we finally pulled up to the store in one piece.

Half an hour later than I'd wanted to.

"Never again," I muttered, jumping into the dusty parking lot.

"No kidding," he muttered right back.

"I told you to let me drive, but no, you wouldn't listen."

Dex slammed his car door shut. "Since you're nagging like we're an old married couple, should I propose now or never?"

"Never," I shot back. "I don't want to spend the rest of my life in jail for killing you to put me out of my misery."

"Aw – I had a moment where I thought it might be nice to marry you. As long as your lips are sewn shut."

"I'll sew your cock to the concrete if you don't be quiet."

He laughed as I pushed open the door to the store. Air con buzzed, all white-noise in the quiet store. Dex followed me in, and I made a beeline for the wiper section. By the time he'd joined me, I'd picked up the one I needed and, for good measure, grabbed a few spares of the ones I knew we'd need again.

I turned and dumped them in the cart Dex had.

He looked at them. "I thought we just needed

one."

I shrugged. "You're the one with a shopping cart."

"I like these places. It's a weakness of mine. What can I say?"

"You have weaknesses? Except your lack of cutting wit, of course."

He clutched his chest. "You wound me, darlin'. And yes, I have weaknesses. For example: I find myself uncomfortably addicted to staring at your ass on a regular basis." He didn't break eye contact as he said that. "And wishing you'd use your mouth to do something else other than talk all the fucking time."

I pursed my lips. I didn't have a response to that—to any of it. The ass thing or the mouth thing.

Especially not the ass thing.

I spun on the balls of my feet and headed down the aisle. I didn't know where I was going, I was just walking in an effort to get away from him.

Holy shit, I still had to get lunch with him.

Yeah. I'd be sitting at a different table.

I liked tacos, and I liked eating them in peace.

And nothing about Dex screamed peace.

"Jamie?" A familiar voice came from the direction of the counter.

I glanced to the side and grinned. "Well I never, Carmella Duvall. What are you doing here?"

My blonde friend pouted and put down her nail file. "I lost a bet."

I laughed. "You know better than to wager on

a shift in this place."

"I know, but Dad called me a chicken shit because I had no money. And you know how well that line always gets me."

"That's why he uses it." I laughed again and hugged her over the counter. "How are you?"

"Good. How are you all doing? I heard your dad's old place is open again."

"Yeah—I'm actually working there."

She frowned. "Awkward?"

"Something like that. He's actually here... somewhere." I looked around, but Dex had disappeared. "Like a kid in a candy store," I muttered. "We only came for wiper blades."

"Supplier back-ordered again?"

"How did you know?" It'd been a problem for longer than Dex knew. And it was always the damn blades...

"How's the new boss?"

"A constant pain in my ass," I admitted. "A total nightmare."

"Ah, look, you're describing yourself again," Dex said from behind me. "You've got to stop doing that."

"I swear to God..." I turned and glared at him.

He grinned. "Are you ready to go?"

I looked at the now-full cart. "Did you buy the entire store?"

"I needed a few things."

"I'm starting to think you didn't make me bring you for the tacos."

"Think what you want. You're being rude." He

nodded toward Carmella.

She offered him a sweet smile. "I've seen her naked. It's all good."

Dex stilled and looked at me. "Is *that* why you're single?"

"I was four," I said dryly. "Sorry to disappoint."

He glanced down at my chest. "I'm undecided on the disappointed thing."

"I swear I will hit you."

"Why don't I take those and scan them for you, Mr...?" Carmella interjected and gave me a "calm down" look.

She knew my temper.

I took a deep breath.

"Dex," he said. "Mr. Ryne is my father."

"You got it, Dex. Get them up here on the counter and I'll scan them through for you. What brought you here then?" She grabbed the first thing and scanned.

"The garage." He glanced at me. "My grandfather bought it and told me to run it before I knew what had hit me."

"Me. I'll be what hits you," I muttered.

He coughed, rubbing his jaw, but I saw the glint in his eye. "I ended up with this one as my employee, and I think I found a gray hair this morning."

"You should dye it again," I said without missing a beat.

Carmella cleared her throat. She was fighting a smile. "Well, good for you, Dex. And I think you'll be presently surprised with Jamie as your employee. She's the best mechanic I know."

*Aw, shucks…*

"So she's trying to prove." His tone was wry, and so was his smile. "How much is that?"

Carmella told him the total and he handed her his card. She wiped and printed the receipt for him to sign. He did so, taking the card back.

"Thank you." She took it with a flourish and dropped the pen into its pot. "Well, Jamie, it was great to see you. Don't be a stranger again. And it was a pleasure to meet you, Dex. Good luck." She offered him a wry smile with a simple twist of her lips, got up, and disappeared into the back room.

He looked at me. "Do you think she'd work reception since you won't?"

I said nothing. I simply stared for a second, then walked out of the store.

He would be the death of me.

# 10

## JAMIE

"I have a question." Dex slid his coffee mug across the table and grabbed a napkin. He wiped his mouth, and then said, "Why does everyone seem to wish me good luck where you're concerned?"

I brought my own mug to my lips and shrugged, giving him my best innocent look. "I have no idea." I sipped.

"Haley mentioned something about a temper."

"She's a terrible over exaggerator." I set my mug down.

"She said it was worse than your attitude."

I rolled my eyes. "Of course that's not true. How could it possibly be?"

He stared at me. "You make an excellent point. But, in the same vein, I can see how you'd have a bad temper."

"I do not have a bad temper," I huffed. "I have a hot temper, and it's a work in progress. Controlling it is a bit like herding cats. Just when

I think I have my ducks in a row, I realize they're more like rabbits at a rave."

"I don't know what I'm more impressed with. Your admission to having a bad temper or your totally ridiculous usage of three animals in a sentence that, weirdly enough, made sense."

"I don't have a bad temper. It's a hot temper. And you're coming dangerously close to being the match that sets it alight."

He leaned forward, eyes twinkling. "Is your temper the only thing I'm setting alight?"

"That was the worst line I've ever heard."

"Impossible. It wasn't a line, it was a genuine question."

"Believe me, I have a whole bunch of things you're setting alight, but none of them are on the same road your thoughts are going down."

"Is there a chance your thoughts are male and can't follow directions?"

I stared flatly at him. Then, picked up my coffee and sipped. I kept my hard stare until my mug clinked against the table once again.

Dex's lips twitched. "I sense a sarcastic comment coming my way."

"As opposed to my regular, non-sarcastic additions to our conversations."

His mouth formed a full grin, one that shone in his eyes. "Ah, there it is. Has anyone ever told you that you're pretty when you cut someone with your words?"

"Now you're just fucking with me." I gave him a pointed look right as the waitress showed up with our tacos.

"Uh," she said uncertainly. "I have our taco sharing platter?"

"Put it right in the middle," Dex said, taking control. "Thank you. And excuse her. She forgot the soap when she brushed her teeth this morning."

My jaw dropped, but the waitress just giggled.

"Is there anything else I can get you both?" she asked Dex.

"Yes. I'd like some water, please," I said to the back side of her head.

"You got it, ma'am."

Jesus, she didn't even look at me as she walked off.

Dex snorted. "It's almost as I answered in your voice without moving my lips."

"You're magic." I selected a taco from the huge-ass board between us and set it on my plate.

"Which one should I start with?" he waved his hand over the platter.

"Hmm. That one." I pointed to the one I had on my plate. The waitress brought over my water, and after a dazzling smile from Dex, left with a blush.

I barely resisted rolling my eyes. Instead, I decided to fold up my taco and shove it in my mouth in a very unladylike way.

But, hey, was there a ladylike way to eat tacos? I hadn't found it yet.

Dex raised an eyebrow, but he didn't say anything, deciding to eat his own lunch. I couldn't say I wasn't glad about it, but I wasn't ready for the deep groan that escaped him when he was halfway through the taco.

"This is a good taco," he said with a mouthful of food.

I hid my smile behind my hand since I, too, had a mouth full of food.

After that, neither of us said a word. It was weird since there hadn't yet been a time—in the staggering number of days we'd worked together—that we'd been quiet, really. Certainly not like this. We'd basically bickered our way through work to this point.

Hell, we'd bickered our way through the entire day so far. It was like we didn't know how to do anything but, and I was okay with it. If bickering with him meant I got to win this stupid thing in the end, I'd take it.

A part of me wanted to make a quip about that, but the rest of me was, well, hungry.

And quite enjoying sitting here without either of us fighting.

Huh.

I had to eat quicker. Hunger was addling my brain.

---

The next morning rolled around too quickly. After lunch yesterday, Dex and I had settled into being almost friendly with each other. I doubted it'd stay the same today, and a part of me was happy about that.

Being nice to each other was weird.

Like...I didn't know how not to snark at him, and I think I'd gone an entire hour without doing it yesterday.

My mom had insisted that was called being an adult. I told her to come and meet Dex and see how 'adult' she expected me to be.

As it was, this morning, I pulled into the parking lot next to his technologically behind truck and got out. It wasn't likely that I'd be able to keep up being nice to him today, but I was willing to try.

Maybe.

It depended on what kind of mood he was in.

I grabbed my purse and walked toward the garage. The doors were open, and there was a strange, high-pitched sound that was either a cat dying or Dex whistling.

I had to vote on the cat.

Dex didn't whistle. Did he?

My steps faltered. I wasn't a big fan of dying cats or whistling. But, I had to admit I was intrigued. What the hell was he whistling for? And was he whistling *Singing in the Rain?*

That had to be the most random thing ever.

I slowly walked under the big doors, dipping my head so I didn't hit them. My sneakers squeaked against the floor, but Dex didn't turn around once. He had a car jacked right up onto axle stands and was lying on the floor under it, something that made the whistles echo off the cold floor.

I put my purse on the coffee table and moved to get a coffee. Shoving my mug under it, I pressed the button and the machine whirred to life, spitting the dark liquid into my "Before coffee, you fucoffee" mug.

Dex's whistling reached me here, especially when the coffee machine was done. I couldn't help the quirk of my lips as I finished making my drink and turned back toward the garage.

He had no idea I was here.

I leaned against the doorframe and pulled the strap of my denim dungaree shorts up over my shoulder. From where I stood, I had an almost perfect view of Dex.

Of the way his arm muscles flexed as he worked on the underside of the car.

I sipped my coffee. It was easier to swallow that than the little lump that was forming in my throat at the sight of him working.

Freaking hell. The car was up high enough that I could see his entire body. His uniformed shirt of a light-colored tank top had ridden up his body, allowing me a sneaky peek at the tight packs of muscle on his stomach. A smudge of grease ran along his hipbone and over the waistband of his light-blue, jean shorts.

My God, what was I doing? Why was I staring all over him like he was a chocolate cake? Was my next move to grab a knife and slice into him?

I shook my head and averted my eyes from him. There was nothing good that would come from staring at him. The only thing that would happen would be an awkward increase in how much I was attracted to him.

Why couldn't he be ugly?

Why were the assholes all hot?

Had I done something terrible in a past life?

I sighed into my mug. My gaze found its way back to him. He reached out one arm, and as he patted around the floor for a tool, his arm flipped this way and that, revealing thick veins running down his forearm.

*Sweet baby Jesus.*

I drained the rest of my coffee, ignoring how hot it was, and refilled the cup. I'd woken up with barely any time to get dressed and braid my hair, so the lack of coffee had to be why I was suddenly turning into a googly-eyed idiot.

That, and I was most definitely an arm girl before anything else.

Hmm... I wondered if duct-taping his mouth would take the asshole out of him?

I shook my head and stirred the cream into my coffee. I definitely needed more caffeine. Next up: some sense knocked into me.

Moving back into the garage, I saw that Dex was still feeling around on the floor for something.

"You know," I said, walking over to where he was working, "if you actually looked for what you wanted instead of blinding flailing around, you might have some success."

"When did you get here?"

I crouched down and peered under the car.

"Sometime between the cat dying and the seagulls protesting."

"Funny. Can you get me the next size down for whatever this one is?" He waved a wrench at me.

I took it from him and checked the size, then did the same to the tools on the floor. "There's a reason you can't find it." I put my coffee down and went to the toolbox where they all were. "You didn't get it out."

"Fuck it."

"Here." I bent back down and handed it to him. "What are you doing?"

"Replacing the transmission. Woman said she was coming down a country road at the speed limit and there was a blind dip. Bunch of scaffolding planks in the road and she hit them at full speed." He shook his head. "She stopped and got the company's name, but it's fucked her gearbox, her suspension, her wheel arches...It won't be cheap."

"Is she sending them the bill?"

"No. I told her I can't do the work without payment because of the cost of parts. She's paying for it, then making a claim to the company."

"Well, that sucks." I sat on a stack of breeze blocks, nursing my cup. "Hey, hasn't this been out in the lot for a few days?"

Dex nodded and removed the transmission mount. I leaned forward and took it from him, placing it out of his way. There was a huge crack in it.

She must have really hit those planks.

"Thanks," he said. "Yeah, it has been. She brought it in last week to get it checked over just in case of damage. She wasn't happy she had to leave it."

I wouldn't be either. "What did her insurance company say?"

"They leased her a car, but it took them two days. That's what she told me when I called and told her the parts had arrived."

"Oh, there was a delivery?"

"No wiper blades. Or wipers, for that matter. Don't get *your* hopes up. I think I'll just call Carmella and start getting them to supply the damn things."

I snorted. "Don't get your hopes up. Carmella is only there when she loses a bet with her family. Jack will be happy to do it though."

He glanced at me, the safety glasses dulling his eyes a little. "I only said Carmella because I thought she worked there."

"Sure you did." I rolled my eyes. "Is there anything else booked in today?"

"Nope." He shot me a devilish smile. "Which means you get to be my glamorous assistant for the day."

I looked down at my clothes. "I'm not exactly Jessica Rabbit over here. My bra might even have an oil stain on. Not so glamorous."

"Might have? Do you need to check?"

"I doubt I care about finding out half as much as you do, Romeo."

Dex laughed. "Worth a try. The idea I might

break you down one day is entertaining."

"To you, perhaps."

He turned to face me with a smirk twisting his lips. "Could you do me a favor and get me a drink? I've been under here forever."

"When you said assistant, I didn't think you meant slave," I said as I got up and walked to the staff area.

"I didn't. And if I did mean slave, running around and doing my bidding isn't the one I'd have in mind!"

I took a deep breath as I poured him water from the filter in the fridge.

What? He didn't specify what he wanted to drink.

I took it back out and crouched again, this time at the front of the car. "Here. Your drink."

He slid out from under it, bringing himself to a stop when he saw what I was holding. "I was about to say that was the quickest anyone's ever made me a coffee, but instead I'm going to say: well played, darlin'. Well played."

I smiled as he sat up and took the glass.

"You know," he said when I stood up, "With that outfit and those braids, all you need is a pair of long socks, and you could be Pippy Long Stocking."

"You know," I said, grabbing my coffee and hitting him with a death glare. "All I'd need is a pair of long socks and you to sit still long enough to make you choke on those words."

A rasping laugh came from the doorway. I

turned to see an older man, presumably in his seventies, standing there, using a walking stick to keep himself upright. His trousers were perfectly pressed, his shoes perfectly shined, and his tan-brown cardigan covered a white-shirt that looked creaseless from where I was standing.

And he bore a very strong resemblance to the man I'd just threatened to choke with a pair of socks.

"You told me she was mouthy," he chuckled. "But you didn't tell me she was owning your ass every time she spoke! No wonder you didn't want to hire her."

I bit the inside of my cheek and looked at Dex for an explanation.

He looked like he'd just walked into the set of a horror movie.

# 11

## DEX

I was an idiot for thinking that my grandpa would never meet Jamie. It'd been wishful thinking—them meeting was the last thing I needed. They would, no doubt, become firm friends.

As his reaction to her had already proven.

What had I done to deserve this hell?

"Pops, this is Jamie. Jamie, this is my grandfather." I waved a hand between them and chugged my water.

Pops glared at me. "Is that how you're gonna introduce me to this lovely young lady? I don't know where I went wrong with you."

I opened my mouth to protest, but he'd already hobbled across the garage to where Jamie was standing and had taken her hand.

"Edwin Ryne," he introduced him, kissing the back of her hand. She blushed. "This uncouth little bastard's grandfather. And you must be the young lady who's got his balls in a twist."

"I'm not listening to this." I got up and walked

away, into the staff area. Why couldn't I have a nice, normal grandfather who was sweet and kind? No wonder I was an asshole. It ran in the damn family.

"That's me," Jamie said, far too happily. "Jamie Bell. It's a pleasure to meet you, sir."

She was so fucking polite. To everyone but me.

"Bell? You wouldn't happen to be related to Simon Bell, would you?"

"Yes, sir. That's my father."

"Would it be remiss of me to welcome you back?"

Jamie laughed softly. "Thank you. It's a little strange."

"No thanks to my grandson, I'd assume."

"There's nothing wrong with me!" I shouted.

"Nothing right, either!" Pops hollered back. "What are you hiding for? Get your ass out here. And bring me a coffee while you're at it."

I rubbed my forehead which quickly moved into me pinching my nose. I took his ornery manner at home—did I have to take this shit at work now, too?

I made the damn coffee and rejoined them. "I was putting my glass in the sink," I replied, ignoring Jamie's smile. "What's up, Pops?"

He rested his mug on his stick. "What are you doing?"

I told him the same story I'd just told Jamie.

He peered over. "That it? Got nothing for Jamie to do?"

"I'm his assistant," she said dryly. "Which

translates to getting him water when he fails to specify what drink he wants."

Pops chuckled. "I like her."

"That's a theme in this family," I muttered.

"What was that?"

"Nothing."

"Why don't you let Jamie do that?" Pops waved at the car.

Oh, Jesus.

"Because I was here first and got started."

"She can finish it."

"Pops..."

"She's got nothing to do."

"I'm sure the phone will ring soon," she said chirpily. "And if it doesn't, he's paying me to basically do nothing, so the joke is on him."

I fucking hated it when she turned shit around so I lost.

"Shit," I whispered.

Jamie grinned, licked her finger, and painted a line in the air like she had the last time she'd outsmarted me.

Two-nil to her.

Three if you counted the tacos, but I wasn't going to give her the satisfaction of that.

Another chuckle escaped Pops. "I really like her."

I pinched my nose again. "Pops. Are you here for a reason other than to embarrass me a little?"

"I embarrass you, huh?" He waggled his gray eyebrows.

"Pops."

He sniffed, sipped his coffee, and said, "It's your aunt's birthday this weekend."

"I'm aware," I said, leaning against the worktop side. "She's left notes on the bathroom mirror every day for the last two weeks with present ideas. This morning, she requested a Ferrari. She can't even drive anymore."

"Yes... She's working hard on that. She asked Roxanne for a hoverboard this morning." Pops paused. "I think she's taking the piss."

"You think?" I said dryly.

"She told me to ensure you both have a date."

I stilled. Nope. That was not happening. I didn't know anyone here well enough except for—

No, fucking hell, no.

Jamie did not need to meet Greta. That would complete my circle of shame because there's no doubt they'd get on like a house on fire.

And I didn't need any of my interactions with Jamie described as a fucking date.

Hell, torture, self-loathing—they worked.

A date?

Fuck no.

"I don't know anyone well enough," I half-lied. "Tell her she'll have to wait until next year."

"You said that last year," Pops pointed out.

"Then we moved."

"Greta won't care."

"I don't care," I said, shaking my head. "Not happening."

Jamie scooted past behind him, carrying her empty mug.

"Jamie! What are you doing this weekend?"

She froze.

"Pops. Don't even think about it!"

"Is your name Jamie, boy? I think not. Jamie?" Pops said, turning to her. "Do you have plans this Saturday?"

"I, er, um." She slowly turned, her eyes wide. "I don't—I'm not sure."

Pops brightened. "Would you like some?"

"Oh fuckin' hell." I lifted the hem of my t-shirt and covered my face with it.

"I don't—uh..."

"Excellent! Dex will pick you up at seven o'clock on Saturday evening. My sister will love you."

"I, er..."

Oh, fucking hell. Fuck, fuck, fucking hell.

This day had started out so well.

"I'll see you for dinner, Dex." Pops hobbled out of the garage. "See you on Saturday, Jamie!"

"Uh..."

When the clicking of his stick had disappeared, I dropped my t-shirt and looked around the garage. Pops had disappeared.

Jamie, however, hadn't. She hadn't even moved. She was still standing in the exact place she had been when Pops had corralled her into coming to the party, but now, she was staring at him with her eyes wide and her lips parted.

Sensing my eyes on her, she turned to face me. "What—what just happened?"

"My grandfather just set us up on a date," I

said tightly.

"Oh no," she breathed. "I think I need to lie down."

That was one way to describe this feeling.

---

"Why would you do this?" I asked, slamming the front door behind me. "Pops!"

"He can't hear you, dear," Aunt Greta called from the kitchen. "He took out his hearing aid because he knew you'd be mad."

"Mad? I'm fucking furious!"

"I'll spray soap in your mouth, boy."

I ground my teeth together and walked into the front room where I knew I'd find him sitting in front of the TV. Must have been fucking interesting if he didn't have the damn hearing aids in.

Just as I'd thought, he was sitting there, feet up on the coffee table, completely oblivious to me. Hell, the damn TV was on silent. He was clearly sitting there for no reason other than to annoy me further.

I snatched the hearing aids from their tray on top of the fireplace and shoved them in front of his face. "Put them on."

He pushed my hand away.

I dropped them on his lap.

He looked up.

"Put. Them. On!" I over-exaggerated my words so he could read my lips. Something I knew he could do because long before he'd accepted he was going deaf, he'd communicated solely through lip-reading.

Pops tapped his ear with one finger and shook his head as if to say he couldn't hear me.

"I know. Put the damn aids in."

He sighed, but put down his little can of beer and fitted both hearing aids. "Yes, boy?"

"What the hell did you do that for?" I didn't miss a beat as I stepped back into my tirade.

"What are you talking about?"

"You know damn well!" I ran my hand through my hair and paced. "Jamie. Why the hell would you force us both into a date neither of us want?"

"She didn't say no." He grinned.

"You have a date?" Greta exclaimed, entering the room with the pace of a drunken turtle.

"Not one I want! Jesus. She's a nightmare. She's too mouthy and sarcastic to make this night enjoyable for even a minute."

"Mouthy and sarcastic?" Roxy said, coming in, too. "You called?"

"See?" I threw my arm in her direction. "We've already got one in attendance. We don't need another!"

"What's going on?"

"He's bringing Jamie to your aunt's party this weekend," Pops answered. "Boy, you're in the way of my TV."

"He is?" Roxy grinned. "You are?"

"Why can't I hear this?" Pops asked.

"It's on mute, you old coot," I said. Turning

to Roxy, I said, "No, I'm not bringing her. Not by choice, at least. This old pain in the ass showed up today and forced us into it."

"She didn't say no. Ah-ha!" Pops clapped when the sound came back on with a boom.

"She didn't fucking say yes!"

"Dexter!" Aunt Greta slapped her hands over her ears. "Turn that racket down, Edwin!"

"Racket? That's a Big Brother replay. No racket at all!" Pops sniffed and settled his hands on his stomach.

Roxy looked between them and motioned for me to follow her. I rubbed my hand over my face and went with her into the dining room.

"Why is he watching Big Brother?" she asked.

"Probably because he couldn't hear it five minutes ago. And to piss off Greta," I grumbled.

Roxy swung out a dining chair and sat down. "Are you really taking Jamie?"

"Where's Charley?"

"In bed. She had McDonald's and fell asleep in the car. Stop avoiding the question."

I pointed at her, then dropped it with a groan. "Yes, I am. I've been forced into it, like she has. He didn't ask. He asked her if she had plans then offered her my plus one. I didn't even want to go as one, never mind a plus one!"

"Is this a bad time to tell you that Mom called me this morning?"

"As a rule, yes."

"She and Dad are flying in tomorrow for Greta's party."

I dragged out a chair and dropped onto it. "No, no, please no."

She grimaced and nodded.

"Fucking hell!" I got up and kicked the chair back under less than ten seconds after I'd sat down. Not that I didn't love seeing my parents, but this was turning into a motherfucking mess.

Roxy laughed. "It's not a big deal, Dex. You're just pissed at Pops for backing you into a corner."

"No, I'm not. I'm pissed at the who."

"Because she doesn't take your shit?"

"No. She's a fucking nightmare. She's fucking insufferable, Rox. She grinds on me like nobody I've ever met in my goddamn life, and the last thing I want is to have to pretend I like her around our family."

My sister raised one dark, slim eyebrow. "I don't know. It sounds to me like she grinds on you because you like her."

I held a finger up at her. "Don't you dare."

"Oh, come on. She's beautiful. You have to admit that."

I said nothing. I didn't need to agree with my sister for that fact to be true. Jamie was beautiful, no doubt about it. Frizzy hair and all.

Roxy laughed. "God, Dex, you're so blinded by your fake hatred you can't even admit that. She's beautiful, she's kickass, and she doesn't cower to your stupid little ideas. Personally, I think you should marry her immediately."

"Fuck, all right, she's beautiful. There. Are you happy?" I threw my arms up. "I can appreciate that, but that doesn't mean I like her."

"You're right, it doesn't. Your insistence that you hate her makes me think you do actually like her."

I ran my hand through my hair again, this time, tugging lightly on it. "I don't like her. I'm attracted to her, and that makes this awkward as fuck. I don't want to be attracted to her or think of her as anything other than the biggest pain in the ass since a colonoscopy."

"That's one helluva way to refer to a woman, I have to admit."

"You're about to join her, Rox!"

My sister fought her amusement for all of five seconds. "Oh my God. I love you. You're so angry at yourself it's comical."

"I'm glad my frustration is amusing to you, *sis*." I made my way toward the dining room door, but she was closer and beat me to it.

She flattened herself against it and shook her head. "I think your problem is that she's nothing like you thought. It's been, what? Four? Five days? And you're already eating your words, brother. Face it: you know she's beautiful. She's strong and independent, and you thought she'd roll over within a day, but she's standing toe-to-toe with you. She's proving you wrong and you hate it."

My jaw twitched.

"And to make matters worse," she smirked, "you want her, and you can't do anything about it because you know she'd introduce her knee to your little boy parts."

"If you refer to my cock as that again, I will smash your new makeup palette with my hammer."

Her jaw dropped. "Sometimes I think you're thirteen," she hissed.

"Sometimes you act like it," I snapped back.

The door yanked open. The swift movement sent Roxy flying backward, and only her quick reflexes as she grabbed hold of the doorframe stopped her from landing on her ass.

Greta looked down at her then up at me. "Your dinner is ready. And you both act like gosh darn thirteen-year-olds. Shut your mouths and come eat."

No matter how pissed I was, nobody disobeyed her when she spoke to you like that.

# 12

## JAMIE

"It's not that bad," Haley said, stroking my hair. "At least you have a date?"

I turned my face to the side so I no longer had a mouthful of pillow. "Hales, in a few hours, I have to get dressed for a party and be surrounded by my sworn enemy's family. It's terrible. Deplorable. I want to run away."

"Has anyone ever told you that you're pretty dramatic?"

"Yes. You, all the time." I shifted and sat up with a huff. "I couldn't even say no. His grandpa backed me into a corner and left before I could do a thing. I swear we didn't say a word to each other the entire day yesterday. He even told me to take today off because it was so fucking awkward."

"Obviously, you obliged. Which explains the homeless person look."

She called it homeless person, I called it mechanic off-duty. In other words, all my clothes were stained with something you could find in a repair shop, and I was okay with that.

It'd been so normal for so long.

"What am I gonna do, Haley? This evening is going to be hell. The only time we've ever been nice to each other is when we got tacos."

"Oh, oh! Did you take him to the place by the auto store?"

I nodded. "We needed wiper blades and I said tacos and he was all over that like a kitten with a yarn ball."

She tapped her finger against her lips. "If you dressed up like a taco…"

"Do not finish that sentence. Ugh." I slid down my bed and crossed to my closet. "What am I even supposed to wear? It's an eightieth birthday party. Cocktail-style attire for dinner followed by dancing."

"Eighty-year-olds still dance?"

I narrowed my eyes as the memory of Dex's grandfather came to mind. "In that family, I'm going to say they can probably bust out the Macarena better than anyone else."

"Hm." She joined me. "Just wear a nice dress and some heels. Do your hair—well, do it as well as you can. And hey, if he's that annoying, use it to torture him a little."

"Torture him? I'm pretty sure I do that every day I show up to work."

She snorted. "Didn't he make an asshole comment about red lipstick?"

"He was amazed I wore lipstick while I

worked."

"So, wear all red." She nudged me out of the way and rifled through my dresses. I didn't have many, given that I was almost always in gym gear or shorts to work in, but the dresses I did have flattered me.

So, her plan was a little terrifying.

I wanted to get through the night, not perform some weird type of seduction on Dex Ryne.

"This one." Haley threw a red dress at me. "I promise you'll survive the night if you wear this."

I held it up. The neck was low but not indecent—perfectly suitable for an elderly party— and I knew the skirt was knee-length and flirty.

"Fine. What shoes?"

She bent down and searched the few shelves that housed my small shoe collection. "These." She tossed me a pair of strappy, black heels. "This purse." A black clutch went flying over her shoulder, and I had to step to the side so she didn't hit me in the head with it. "And your leather jacket. Perfect. Edgy yet feminine."

The leather jacket landed on my bed. I dropped the dress on top of it and stepped back. I wasn't sure. The only time I'd ever been dressed up around him was when I'd had my interview, and that didn't really count. That was formal, not fancy, and there's a big difference between those two things.

Haley stared at me. "You're questioning everything, aren't you?"

I didn't need to reply for her to know that I

was right.

"Just call and don't go. You don't like him, and you're only going because you were talked into it. Neither of you would have agreed to this otherwise."

"I know, but his grandpa was kinda sweet. If pushy," I acquiesced. "But still, sweet."

"So, go with his grandpa." She snorted. "God, Jamie. This is ridiculous, do you know that?"

"Yes. If I didn't think it was, we wouldn't be having this conversation right now, would we?" I dropped my ass onto the bed. "God, the idea of this is painful. I can't tolerate him for an hour. How am I supposed to pretend to be his date?"

"Can. Cal," she said. "Cancel. Boom. Easy. "Sorry. My best friend's hamster died and she needs me tonight."'"

"That's not even remotely believable," I replied. "I just have to suck it up, don't I?"

"Suck what up?" my mom asked as she stepped into my bedroom.

"Hi, Mom. I really appreciate you knocking!"

She waved her hand and glanced at the bed. "Oooh. Do you have a date?"

A mischievous grin crossed Haley's face. "Yeah, with her boss."

"The sexist guy who didn't want to hire you?" Mom threw her attention all my way. "How the hell did that happen?"

I explained, begrudgingly, how his grandfather had tricked us into it.

"A man with a plan. I like that. What are you

wearing?"

"Ooh!" Haley clapped her hands together. "So, she has the red dress because red is her thing."

"Absolutely. And it works so well with her coloring."

"Right. The shoes because they're to die for."

"Gorgeous."

"The clutch because simple is best."

"Agreed."

"And the leather jacket to remind him that while she's beautiful, she's also one badass bitch and will still stick her stiletto into his balls."

Mom clapped her hands together the way Haley had just minutes ago. "Perfect. What's she doing with her hair?"

"Trying her best," Haley said ruefully.

I touched the frizzy mess that was my hair. Geez. We didn't all have perfect, straight hair.

Mom sighed and nodded. "I wonder if there's a home remedy for frizzy hair we have time to make."

"Ooh! Let's go and look!"

Just like that, my mom and best friend skipped off without a second of input from me.

"That's it, guys," I muttered, picking up one of the—undeniably pretty shoes—and looking at it. "That's how we battle sexism. We don't prove them wrong, we show up looking pretty and smile."

Then, I threw the shoe at the closed door and dropped back onto the bed to stare at my ceiling until they decided it was time to manhandle my

127

hair to their satisfaction.

---

All right. I didn't have to like it, but the olive oil and avocado mask I'd been made to slather on my hair and sit in for an hour or so had worked.

It wasn't perfect, but with some a skilled blow dry from Haley and a joint effort at running the straightening iron over my hair—twice—it actually resembled loose waves instead of...a conductor for an electrical current.

And I looked good, too. Haley had nailed the outfit. Not that I'd admitted that, lest she got ideas for the future. If she had even an inch of knowing she'd been right, she'd be rifling through my entire wardrobe by the time I got home.

As for now, I was tugging uncomfortably on the collar of my leather jacket, standing in the middle of my living room. I wanted to pace, but if I did, I knew my feet would kill within the next hour.

I was antsy. I didn't want Dex to see me like this. I didn't know why, just that this whole night added a dynamic to our relationship—one there was no place for.

The sound of a car pulling up on the gravel drive outside my house drew my attention out of my head and to outside. I peeked between the blind and looked out.

Dex's truck stopped, the lights illuminating the driveway. It was that weird, dusky time where the sun couldn't decide it if were up or down, and I was glad I didn't have to drive, I had to be honest.

I drew in a deep breath as three, loud knocks sounded on my door. Steeling myself, I let it go and opened the door.

He stood in front of me, looking like a completely different person. He still had that five o'clock shadow over his jaw, but his hair was slicked back and held in place by wax or gel or something.

A bright, white shirt stretched across his body, and the top two buttons were open, giving me the hint of a glance at his collarbones at the base of his neck. I sent my gaze down to where his shirt sleeves were rolled just above his elbows, leaving me a full view of those veiny forearms of his.

It was tucked into a pair of dark jeans that hid suede, dark brown boots.

And he was...clean.

So was I.

Miracles did happen.

Dex shifted uncomfortably on my doorstep. He kept looking at me and glancing away, and he brought his hand up to his hair only to stop and drop it again.

"Hey," he said after a long moment of us both looking to the side awkwardly. "You look..."

I waited for him to finish, and when he didn't, I fought a smile. "Wow, you know how to compliment a girl."

He grimaced. "Would you believe I practiced

telling you look beautiful just to be a good date?"

"Not in the slightest." I hid a laugh. "You don't have to pretend to be a good date. Neither of us want to be here. Let's just focus on getting through the night without killing each other."

"Sounds like a plan to me." He glanced at my feet. "I will help you get in the truck, though, because if you break your neck in those things, I'm the one who'll get the blame."

I snatched my clutch from the windowsill and stepped out onto the doorstep right next to him. As I locked the door, I said, "I can climb into your truck, Dex. I don't need you to throw a rope down to help me."

"Actually, I was going to give you a hand in the hopes I could touch your ass."

"And there he is." I checked my phone when I tucked my keys away. "Five minutes before you let your inner jackass out. Go you."

"I try," he admitted, stepping onto the gravel. "Come on." He walked to his truck and opened the door.

"Hold on." I held up a finger as I drew level with him. "Ground rules, since you're already being a dick."

He sighed. "I can assure you I'll be doing everything possible not to talk to you tonight. You don't need rules."

I raised my eyebrows. "One," I said. "If you must touch me under the guise of being a gentleman—"

He snorted.

"—then you can touch my hands, my waist, or my back. If you touch anything else, even knock my foot with yours under the table, I will junk-punch you."

"I'll do my best not to touch you at all. I can't think of anything worse."

"Two." I held up two fingers. "If you mention anything about me being inferior to you at work, I will junk-punch you."

"I'll make sure you're out of earshot when I do."

"Three." A third finger went up. "I don't have a third, but I don't think I need one."

He held his hands up. "You've got a deal. I happen to like my junk, and I don't want it to get hurt anytime soon."

I rolled my eyes and slipped past him, only just brushing up against him as I did. He stepped back muttering under his breath, and I hauled myself up into the cab.

"Hey...You said I can't touch. Does that mean I can look?"

I slammed the truck door.

He held up three fingers and nodded.

There was point three.

Not that it would stop him if he really wanted to, but still.

I needed those points in place.

# 13

## DEX

Don't touch.
Don't talk.
Don't look.
The first two? Doable.
The last?
Fuck me dead and serve me on a platter—that was impossible.

How the fuck was I supposed to not look at her? If she was beautiful in denim shorts and covered in oil, she was fucking beyond that dressed the way she was right now.

That jacket. That dress. Those shoes.
Her.

I rubbed my hand across my face as I got out of the truck. It was dark in the parking lot of the bar-restaurant, and thank fuck for that. I needed to take a moment and compose myself.

If she smart-mouthed me tonight when she looked like that, I wouldn't be able to resist her.

And shit, if she kissed with the passion she cut me down, it'd be worth the junk-punch.

No doubt about it.

"All right," she said, smoothing down her dress. She pushed the door shut with one flick of her wrist. "Let's get this over with."

"I'm so glad to see we share the same sentiments over this." I stopped just outside the door. "Oh, by the way, you have to take my arm. My mother will give birth to an elephant if she sees me being an ass."

"Then you should call the zoo, because she's about to birth a herd."

I sighed. "Please?"

"Fine, but you owe me."

"I don't like the sound of that."

"You're not supposed to." She flashed me the biggest playful grin I'd ever seen cross her face and took my arm. "Are your parents...like your sister and grandpa?"

Translation: were they as unfiltered as the members of my family she'd already met?

"Absolutely. You will love them. My mother will spend the entire evening chastising me and Pops while Dad laughs, Greta tells her to lighten up, and Roxy films the entire thing."

"Sounds like a riot."

"Wait 'til the oldies get the whiskey out."

"I've never seen any of the old people here drink whiskey."

"Who doesn't drink whiskey?" Aunt Greta asked from the bar.

Here we go.

Hell had officially opened its gates.

"Great Aunt Greta, this is Jamie. Jamie, this is my great aunt." I introduced them.

Greta peered at her with narrowed eyes. "Jamie. You're the one keeping him on his toes at work, aren't cha?"

I really wished everyone would stop saying that. It wasn't fucking true.

Jamie, however, beamed the way she did every time she heard it. "Yes, ma'am, that's me."

"Good. You keep that shit up."

Jamie paused, shocked. "You got it."

"Did you tell her it's my birthday?" Aunt Greta looked at me.

"Yes, I did," I ground out.

"But I'm afraid I'm empty handed, because I didn't get much notice. But I'd love to buy you a drink to wish you happy birthday." Jamie stepped next to her at the bar. "What would you like, ma'am?"

She was such a suck-up.

Greta looked at me with an 'ooh' expression. "I'll take a shot of whiskey, dear, and you will, too."

"Greta..."

"Two shots of whiskey, please," Jamie said, putting a ten on the bar.

The bartender nodded, took the bill, and turned to pour shots.

What had I done?

"Hooooey," Greta trilled when the shots were

slid in front of them. "Are ya ready, Jamie? Let's go! One, two, three!"

They both threw them back. Greta barely flinched, but Jamie scrunched her shoulders up to her ears and shuddered. I coughed to hide my laugh, especially when she turned and her face was all wrinkled up, too.

Greta grinned. "Few more of those and you won't notice it, my girl." She waved a finger for the bartender.

"Are Mom and Dad here yet?" I asked, grabbing Jamie's wrist.

It was close enough to her hand...

"Not yet. But your sister is, and your grandfather is telling stories about the war to the boys at the poker table."

"Awesome. We'll see you back there." I steered Jamie away from her before she could ply her with another shot before she'd eaten anything.

Jamie laughed. "Wow. She's...something."

"That's the most accurate explanation of her I've ever heard," I muttered. "And why the hell is there a poker table?"

"I was hoping you could answer that," she said when I released her wrist.

I caught sight of Roxy waving from the far corner. "If only. There's Roxy. Let's go." I nudged her back in that direction, and she started walking.

"Hey!" Roxy grinned and squeezed Jamie's arm when she sat down.

Oh God, was she tipsy?

This was a mess.

"Have you been drinking already?" I asked, taking the seat opposite her and next to Jamie.

Roxy leaned forward. "Yes. Greta is peddling the shots."

"I know." Jamie screwed her face up.

My sister giggled. "She got you already, huh?"

"She offered to buy her a drink." I leaned back and folded my arms. "Rookie error."

"Shouldn't you be buying your date a drink?" her eyes glittered as she said it.

"It's not a date," me and Jamie said together.

"Don't make me tell Mom."

I stood up and kicked my chair aside. "I hate you. Jamie? What would you like to drink?"

"Pinot Grigio is fine. I can give you the—"

"Please don't give her ammunition to tattle on me. It's been her favorite game for years. I'll buy it." I held up my hand and, shaking my head, left and returned to the bar.

A different area to where my aunt was. I did not need to get suckered into whiskey shots, mostly because I had to get Jamie home safely.

I ordered her wine and myself a Coke, paid, and took them to our table in the corner. I noticed that Roxy had cleverly picked a four-seater table to stop any of our family from joining us to eat.

She wasn't always smart, but when she was...

"Here." I put the wine in front of Jamie and sat back down.

Roxy looked at me. "You didn't buy your sister a drink?"

I paused, and then, "No. I'm not going to be

responsible for you getting drunk before our parents have even shown up."

"Oh, God." She pressed her hand to her face. "Shit, they're here. Be right back. I'm going to find water." She got up and scooted past me, only just wobbling a tiny bit.

"Is she all right?" Jamie asked, watching after her with a twist to her lips.

"Fine. She just realized Mom will side-eye her all night if she's already drunk. Now, quick, move into her seat, or else we'll get blindsided by my family."

"I can't steal her seat!"

"Sure you can. You snooze, you lose in this family." I moved to sit opposite her. "It's either you move or you can stare into my eyes all night."

"Ugh." Jamie moved, and I bit back a laugh.

I peered over at her as she sipped her wine. She looked really different tonight, and not just because she was dressed up. No, there was something I couldn't put my finger on exactly.

"Stop staring at me," she muttered.

"You look different," I said quietly. "It's weird."

"Is that the compliment you forgot to give me earlier?"

I dipped my head and smiled. "No. I'm still figuring out how you look so different. I'll look at you and make you uncomfortable for a couple hours while I figure it out."

"I'd really rather you didn't." She held her glass to her mouth. "Why is your aunt walking around with a huge tray of shots?"

I jerked my head around to where, shit, she was right. This entire area had been marked off for her private party, and Greta was going from table to table with a tray of whiskey shots.

"Is this what you meant when you said she'd corrupt everyone with whiskey?"

I took a deep breath and nodded as a table of elderly people at the blackjack table grabbed one each. "Yep. She's a whiskey peddler. It's terrifying. She can get anyone drunk."

"So, avoid the birthday girl."

"That will never happen," Roxy slipped into the seat Jamie had just vacated. "I see we're playing musical chairs."

Jamie sipped. "He made me do it. Oh no, she's coming."

Thankfully, Greta's arrival made my sister forget we'd just moved seats.

"Shots!" She put three on the table, and before any of us could say a word, she was gone.

Jamie let out a long breath. "This is going to be a long night."

I looked over at her.

She had no idea.

---

"That fourth shot was a bad idea." Jamie sipped her water. "She could talk a pig into a visit to the slaughterhouse."

I laughed and leaned right back. We'd stayed in our corner table long after my parents had arrived, introduced themselves, and we'd eaten. Roxy had disappeared to play poker not long after dinner, and Greta had caught on to Jamie not taking her shots.

She'd stood in front of the table with her own until Jamie gave in.

She'd been drinking spritzers to make up for it.

"She could talk an entire farm into a visit there," I corrected her. Her cheeks were flushed from both the alcohol and the heat, and she looked fucking adorable.

The bonus? She'd only threatened to punch me in the balls once. It was in front of my parents. My mom had laughed, while Dad agreed I deserved it.

I didn't mean to say she shouldn't be in my garage. It just kinda...slipped out.

Roxy came dancing over to us, pointing at Jamie with alternating hands.

"No." Jamie held her hands out. "No. No. No."

"Yes, yes, yeeeeees!" Roxy grabbed her hands and pulled her out of the seat.

"Help," Jamie mouthed, looking over her shoulder at me as my sister pulled her onto the dancefloor.

I laughed and just watched as she went. Her plea didn't last long as Roxy twirled her around, laughing her ass off. I couldn't stop myself from laughing, either. They were surrounded by, pretty much, old people who were moving slower than a snail as they danced, and Jamie looked so awkward.

Roxy was so drunk she didn't care, but not so drunk she was out of control. My sister was someone who didn't really care what people thought in general, and despite what Jamie said, I knew they were total opposites.

Which made their newfound friendship a little hard to understand.

Jamie cared what other people thought.

That's why she was here in the first place.

She cared about proving she was good at what she did.

I tilted my head to the side and watched as she slowly gave in to the music—and my sister—and danced.

Jamie cared enough that she'd come here tonight when she didn't have to. That she'd spent the entire night with me when there were a hundred other things I knew she could have been doing.

Roxy looked over at me and winked.

I immediately looked away.

Shit. She'd caught me staring at Jamie. Now I was never going to hear the end of it from her.

"She's pretty, huh?" Dad took the seat next to me and pushed his glasses up his nose.

"Dunno who you're talking about." I drank my Coke.

He laughed. "Jamie. Your grandfather has been telling me all about her."

"You know he's crazy, right?"

"She's pretty, she's got your number..."

I sighed. "If everyone in this family could stop marrying me off to the person who hated me on sight, that would be great."

"She hated you on sight, huh?"

"It was mutual."

"That's how me and your mother met," he mused. "I'd just accidentally hit a baseball through the passenger side window of her brand-new car. Two days after she moved in across the street."

I slid my gaze toward him. "That's a new story. How didn't we know that?"

"Well, son, let's face it. You can be a bit of an ass sometimes."

"Thanks, Dad."

"So, I was saving it for a moment just like this."

I gave him a thumb up and looked back out at the dancefloor. Both Roxy and Jamie had disappeared, and that spelled disaster.

"Someone needs to take that tray from Greta."

I jerked my head around. Dad was right—Greta still had a tray, or rather, she'd commandeered someone to handle it for her.

"Dad. I think we're up."

Dad sighed, but we both stood and crossed the room to where Greta was drunkenly peddling shots to... Roxy and Jamie.

They both took one before we had a chance to get to them and stop them.

"I'll take that." Dad took the tray from the old guy who held it and swept it straight to the bar.

Greta held her finger up and shrieked Dad's

name before dragging her poor new friend behind her.

Roxy snorted. "I need the bathroom. I'll be right back." She waved at us and headed in the direction of the bathrooms.

"I thought you said she was a whiskey peddler," I said to Jamie, half-grinning.

She pressed her hands against her cheeks. "She is. It's crazy. She shoves it at you and stares at you and woosh, you're a goner!"

Laughing, I handed her her purse. "Here. I didn't want to leave it at the table."

"Thanks." She unclipped the top and pulled out a chain strap before doing it back up. She threw the strap over her head, across her body, and grabbed my hand. "Dance?"

"I don't dance."

"Neither do I."

"I've just watched you for the last fifteen minutes. You definitely do dance."

She stopped in the middle of the floor, eyebrow quirked and lips curling. "You watched me, did you?"

"Not specifically. I mean, I could see you. It's not like you were a TV or anything."

She giggled behind her hand. "You're so awkward."

I'd been called many things, but awkward wasn't one of them.

"I think you need some fresh air." I grabbed hold of her arms and steered her toward the back doors. "And I'm aware this is outside of your safe touching zone, but it's for your own good."

More laughter escaped her. "I'm fine. I'm just in a good mood."

"Huh. That's why I think you're hammered. I've never seen you in one of those."

She looked at me over her shoulder as she sat on one of the benches in the side garden. "You're such a charmer."

"I've been nice all night. It's all built up, and here we go. I'm charming the panties off you."

"I doubt that. You'll say one thing too far and whoosh." She made a sweeping movement through the air with her hand. "They'd be clamped on with a coded padlock."

I laughed as I sat with her. "There's the Jamie I know. She's under the whiskey and dancing."

"Careful. I'm keeping her on a tight rein." She tapped a finger against her chin.

And I knew.

I knew what was so damn different about her.

It was her freaking hair.

"Your hair," I muttered, my fingers twitching.

"What?" She did a double-take and touched it. "Is something wrong with it?"

"No." My lips tugged at the sides. "It's what's making you so different. You don't look like you stuck your finger into a plug socket."

She pressed her hand to her mouth. "I can't even be mad about that. It's true."

"How did you do it?" I reached over and tugged the end of a wavy lock.

"I didn't. My best friend and mom did." She

untucked it from her ear, letting it fall over her face.

"Don't. Untuck it. I mean." I hesitated only a second before I reached out and pushed it back behind her ear. It was soft and smooth, a world away from its usual state, and I let my fingers run through it to the very ends.

Our eyes were connected the whole time, and my inhale was a little too sharp.

Jamie bit her lip and looked away.

I yanked my hand back and cleared my throat.

"I'm hungry. Let's get some pizza!" She jumped up faster than she should have been able to in those shoes and, with a good few feet of distance between us, looked at me with her hands clapped together. "Yes? Pizza? Yes?"

She was desperate to break the tension, and as much as I should have said no and taken her home...

"All right. We'll even sneak out the back here, but you have to take me to a decent place."

"As long as you promise to follow directions this time."

"Psst. It wasn't my fault."

# 14

## JAMIE

We both sat on my front doorstep, illuminated by the hallway light thanks to the front door being open. I'd discarded my shoes in the car after we'd bought pizza, and Dex had undone his shirt another button and untucked it.

With the pizza between us, we ate in silence. I didn't know what he was thinking. I'd been all kinds of tipsy before we'd gone outside and he'd tucked my hair behind my ear.

All night.

It'd taken him all night to realize that was what was different about me. Did that mean he'd been looking at me all night to figure it out? Or had he had a lightbulb ping over the top of his head?

Why did it matter? Why did I care?

Oh, because it'd felt damn good when he'd tucked it behind my ear. When he'd forced me to take it off my face, to stop hiding. When he'd run his fingers right through my hair to the tips as he'd looked at me and...

I shoved some of the stuffed crust into my mouth.

I'd known this was a bad idea, and this was why. I knew I'd see him as something more—or that alcohol would do that.

Him touching me had sobered me up in seconds. Pizza had been the best way to disguise that fact.

"So. Your family is crazy."

Dex peered over at me, licking his fingers. "That's one word to describe them."

"No, seriously. I thought my family was insane, and then I met yours."

"Your family sounds perfectly normal as far as I know. Your best friend..." He put out his hand and waved it side to side. "She's a little sketchy."

Well, he wasn't wrong.

"Well, I mean," I paused, putting a bit of stringy cheese into my mouth before swallowing it and continuing. "My parents broke up when I was eight, then my dad remarried, then divorced her last year. My parents got married the week after."

Dex choked on his pizza. "Wait, what?"

"My parents broke up. Then my dad got married again, except she was a gold-digging whore with one hell of a shovel in her ass pocket." I uncapped my bottle of water and sipped, motioning for him to give me a minute. "Long story short, she spent money we didn't have, and that's why my dad had to sell the garage. He divorced her, but it wasn't enough. My parents stayed really good friends, and I guess they fell back in love again."

"Wow. That is crazy." Dex put his half-eaten slice back in the box and licked his fingers again, this time wiping them on his jeans.

I did the same on my clutch.

Hey—a little cheese grease was nothing compared to what we dealt with every day.

"Are you done?" he asked, motioning to the box.

I nodded, cradling my water bottle.

He moved it the box away to the side and rested his elbows on his knees, leaning right forward. "Well, thank you. Tonight was fun. More than I thought it would be."

I propped my elbow on my knee and rested my cheek on my hand. "Me, too. Thank you."

He stood up and held his hands out. I put mine in his, and he wrapped his strong, rough fingers around mine and pulled me up. I staggered a little but steadied myself with a giggle.

"Thanks. So, I'll see you on Monday?" I tugged my hands, but he tightened his grip on them.

"Monday. Bright and early. It's a busy day."

"Perfect."

We shared a smile, and I finally managed to get my hands out of his grip.

He half-turned, then stopped. "Jamie?"

With my fingers through the straps of my shoes, I straightened. "Yeah?"

Dex took a step toward me. "I have something I forgot to tell you."

"Oh?" I looked up with interest. "What's that?"

For the second time tonight, he reached up and tucked my hair behind my ear. I drew in a deep breath, my face tilting into his touch.

"You looked beautiful tonight."

I smiled, laughing softly. "You didn't look too bad yourself. Shit—did I say that out loud?"

Laughing much louder than I had, Dex dropped his hand and stepped back. "You sure did, darlin'." He grabbed the pizza box and backed toward his truck. "Good thing you did. If you hadn't, I'd be kissing you right now."

My lips parted.

His words had sucked the air out of me, and I didn't move, except to breathe, as he got in his truck with a cocky grin. He dumped the pizza on the passenger side seat.

With that grin still in place, he started the engine and reversed down my driveway.

I saw the shadow of that grin—and heard the echo of his words—long after his headlamps had disappeared from my view.

---

I was early.

Only half an hour early, but early all the same. I hadn't even checked my clock when I'd left. I just wanted to get here. Beat Dex to it. Put my head in the right place.

The whiskey had won yesterday morning. I might have been sober by the time I went to sleep, but I'd forgotten to drink water, and I deserved every second of the headache that had plagued me for the entire day.

It'd also done some addling to my thoughts in that I hadn't been able to think about what he'd said. Honestly, I didn't want to. I could take the flippant, off-the-cuff remarks about looking at me, but straight up saying he wanted to kiss me?

Well, hello, inner teenage self. I missed you.

I leaned forward and rested my head on the steering wheel.

I wish he'd just damn well done it. If I was going to overthink this, I may as well have had something tangible to overthink.

Because, yet again, I wished he'd done it. Wished he'd taken the moment and kissed me.

Three times he'd tucked my hair behind my ear.

Twice he'd almost kissed me.

Once, just once, I wanted him to do it.

To get it over with so I'd stop wondering. To get it out of his system if he had to. To kill the elephant that I now knew would be sitting in the corner of the garage until it happened—if it happened.

To kill the tension that would undoubtedly be there, no matter what we did or said.

*Knock. Knock.*

I screamed, sitting back upright and hitting the back of my head on the headrest.

Outside my car, Dex roared with laughter.

I set my jaw and got out. "What the hell? That wasn't funny!"

He leaned back against his truck, clutching his stomach. "Maybe not for you. Were you sleeping?"

"No. I was thinking I'm early and there's no coffee. Now I'm thinking I already want to kill you!" I smacked his arm.

He grabbed my wrist, his lips curving into a half-grin. His shining eyes met mine. "Good morning to you, too."

I snatched my wrist from him. "God, I hate you."

"I know. I get a thrill every time you tell me." He pulled the keys out of his pocket with another laugh. "Come on. If you haven't had coffee, I don't want to talk to you anymore."

I pulled my purse out of my car and locked it. "What the hell is that supposed to mean?"

"I know the answer to that, and it's silence. I've already had that conversation with my still-hungover sister today."

"Oh no." I followed him into the staff area. "That bad, huh?"

"Well, I'd just gotten home when my mom called and said I needed to rescue Roxy. Greta was plying her with shots, and she was so drunk she thought the vodka was water."

I put down my purse. "How do you even mix that up?"

"I think you get so drunk you pass out, but not so drunk you choke on your own vomit." He shrugged and turned on the coffee machine. "It's a miracle she didn't vomit at all, actually."

I winced when he set a cup going and turned around. "That sounds...fun?"

"No. I should have ignored the call and pretended to be asleep."

"There he is. There's the asshole who went missing the entire evening on Saturday."

He grinned, eyes dancing with silent laughter. "I told you, I was behaving. Now, all bets are off."

That sounded like he wasn't just talking about being an asshole.

*Ahem.*

"Well, at least you stuck to the ground rules," I said. "Just."

He folded his arms, gaze locked onto mine. "Are they still in place?"

"Always. Not that you care."

Another grin. "That sounded like permission to break them."

My lips parted. "It was nothing like that!"

He poured cream into the cup and stirred. "Calm down, shrilly pants. I'm fucking with you."

"I will pour that coffee over your head, Dexter Ryne."

"It's kinda hot when you full-name me like that."

I took a deep breath in. One. Two. Three...

"Here." He held out the coffee. "I made you a bitch pill."

I glared at him without taking the mug.

His shoulders trembled as he held in a laugh. "Oh, I'm sorry, my tongue slipped. I meant a coffee."

"One. Two. Three. Four. Five..."

He laughed as I counted under my breath.

"Take it. Come on. It's the last of it and I have to go and get more before I do something stupid." He pushed it closer to me.

I took it. "Thank you. And you assume you haven't already done something stupid."

His gaze dropped to my lips and lingered there for a moment before he raised his eyes back up to meet mine. "Not the kind of stupid I'm talking about."

Once again, he left me speechless and staring after him as he left.

Fucking hell.

---

Wide berth.

Give Dex a wide berth.

That was my plan for today. Don't speak unless necessary, and absolutely do not brush hands in the toolbox again.

Hormonal Jamie had taken over, and Smart Jamie was struggling to take back control from the little hussy.

I wiped the dipstick from the oil and put it back in to check the level. It didn't need much, but since I was here, I'd do it anyway. I grabbed the oil, filled, and rechecked the level.

Dex was still working on the car that had driven over scaffolding planks, which meant I was doing service after M.O.T after service. Not that I minded—it kept me busy, which meant there was less time to bitch with him.

The silence was quite nice, actually.

I ran through the rest of things under the hood for the service, changing where necessary, topping up and tightening various things. It was no more than routine. I leaned right over to the back where the engine coolant was. It was on the minimum level, so I bent down to grab it from the floor so I could fill it.

When I was done, I screwed the cap on both the bottle and the tank.

And paused.

Someone was staring at me.

And there was only one other person in this garage.

I put down the coolant bottle and cleared my throat, then slowly turned my head to look over my shoulder.

Dex stood in the doorway, his tank messed with oil and grime, his hair a sticking-up mess, and his light jeans ripped and dirty. His hands were that awkward stage between "I just washed them" and "This won't come off", something that was only exaggerated by the water bottle he held.

And his gaze was firmly on me.

"Can I help you?" I asked.

He blinked and met my eyes.

"What the hell are you doing over there?" I pushed to stand up straight.

"Right now?" He capped his water bottle. "Well, honestly... I'm just thinking you'd look better over the hood of that car than under it."

I unhooked the hood and slammed it down, spinning on the balls of my feet.

Our eyes met properly. I didn't like what I saw in his—desire, attraction, need. Which was obviously why a shiver ran down my spine.

I cocked a hip, putting my hand on it. "The only time you will ever get me *over* a hood of a car is if a wiper blade needs changing. So, unless you're a wiper blade..."

Dex pulled his phone from his pocket and started tapping the screen.

I blinked. "What are you doing?"

He peered up at me through his unfairly thick eyelashes. "Seeing if I can get a wiper blade costume for Halloween."

"I don't even know how to respond to that."

"You can buy wiper blade glasses."

"What?"

He raised his eyebrows. "And a lady here on eBay will hand-make any costume. There's my Halloween sorted."

I stared at him. "You're not getting me over anything, Dex. Definitely not a car hood. No matter what you think."

He clutched his chest dramatically. "You wound me."

"Unfortunately not fatally," I muttered.

"You also underestimate me."

"There's a lot of that going around in this garage." I put the bottle of coolant away.

"Touché."

"Thank you."

"Can I ask you something?"

I sighed and turned to face him again. "What?"

Earnestly, he asked, "Can you stop wearing those tiny shorts? Or yoga pants that make me want to touch your ass every five minutes?"

I looked down at the ripped shorts of my dungarees. "Can you keep your thoughts to yourself? Control yourself, maybe? Not look at me and see someone worth screwing?"

He licked his lips. "I don't understand the question."

"Oh my God. You're like Jekyll and Hyde, aren't you?" I grabbed a clean town from the shelf and wiped my hands. "I swear, you're two different people. Inside this garage, you're a raging fucking asshole. Outside of it? You're actually a nice person who isn't torturous to spend time with."

"Interesting. I feel the same way about you. Except wanting to kiss you. That doesn't seem to change no matter where we are."

"Yeah, well, you should have done that on Saturday when I actually *wanted* you to, because now the moment's gone."

I froze, halfway through wiping my hands.

Did I just say that?

Aw, shit, I did.

Was there a chance he didn't hear me?

Judging by the way his bright eyes were hot on me, the answer to that was no.

"Never mind," I said quickly. "Slip of the

tongue. I didn't mean to say that. Oh look, it's time for lunch."

I threw the towel to the side and ran past him into the staff room. I grabbed my purse and ran back out, feeling his eyes on me the entire time.

How could I have said that? How could I not have thought that through?

Jesus, the last thing I needed was for him to know I'd wanted him to kiss me. Now, he'd know I'd thought about it. Now, he knew I was attracted to him.

This was a hot mess.

I put my purse on top of my car so I could fumble for my keys. Adrenaline trickled through my veins and my hands shook as I tried to find them.

Finally, my fingers curled around the cold, metal ring full of keys and keyrings.

I was yanked away from my car.

A tiny scream escaped me.

Rough hands framed my face, and all I saw before I was pushed against Dex's truck was a flash of his bright blue eyes.

Before I could ask what he was doing, he kissed me.

His lips were soft, but his kiss was not. Rough and needy, he pinned me to the truck with his solid body as he moved his lips across mine.

A bolt of pure desire shot through me, and my keys fell to the ground. His grip on me was so tight, his body so hard, and Jesus, it felt good.

I'd all but asked for this.

His fingers teased my hair as his tongue teased the seam of my lips. I wound my fingers in the sides of his shirt and gave in. It was a battle I'd lose anyway—one I didn't want to win. Goosebumps were prickling across my skin as our kiss deepened.

This was a mistake, one we'd both regret the second it was over. It was fueled by angry desire and pent-up frustration toward the other. It wasn't romantic or swoony. It was raw, but it felt so damn good I didn't even care.

It felt so damn good, I wanted more.

Dex pulled away first. When his eyes found mine, I saw the battle.

He wanted more, too.

I could *feel* that he wanted more, thanks to the fact his cock was pressing against my stomach.

I wanted to speak, but I couldn't. My lips felt so swollen, like it'd lasted a lot longer than it had.

He pulled his hands away from my face and stepped back, pinching his lower lip. Bending down, he picked up my keys and handed them to me. "Since you're going out...Would you grab me lunch, too?"

I nodded, swallowing.

"Does that taco place do take-out?"

Again, I nodded. I didn't trust myself to speak.

"I'll pay you back when you get back."

This time, I got in my car. I didn't care about that. I recognized the request for what it was, and I appreciated it.

Apart.

We needed to get away from each other, and we needed to do it now.

I started the engine and tore away from the garage before he'd even made it back inside.

# 15

## DEX

I kicked the side of the rolling toolbox and ran my fingers through my hair.

Fuck.

Why the fuck had I done that? I should have just let her go. I had no reason to chase her except for my own selfish desire. No reason to kiss her except I wanted to.

Because she'd admitted she wanted me to.

On *Saturday*.

Not today. Not tomorrow. Hell, not even fucking yesterday. Not even all day Saturday. Just that one, fleeting moment when I should have damn well done it, her smart little mouth be damned.

And fuck, that woman had a fire burning inside her, and it was there when she kissed, too. She didn't hesitate to kiss me back. Didn't stop when she dropped her keys. Her nails had scratched across my skin when she'd grabbed my shirt, and

I still had the fucking goosebumps from that.

I wanted to do it again. Wanted to feel her melt under me while I kissed her.

Which was why I sent her to the taco place. I didn't even want them. I wasn't hungry. I just wanted to put some space between us, because if she came back in five minutes like she normally did, I wouldn't be able to look at her.

What the fuck was I supposed to say to her when she got back?

I wasn't going to apologize. There was no chance in hell I'd be doing that. I couldn't apologize for something I wasn't sorry for.

All right—maybe I was a little sorry for slamming her against the truck, but not for kissing her.

I grabbed a bottle of water from the fridge and drank half of it. My heart was still thumping against my ribs, and fuck if I hadn't wanted to grab hold of her and carry her inside.

How the hell was I supposed to get rid of this rush?

That's what it was. I'd kissed her once, and it was nothing but a rush. Like adrenaline but better. Potentially more addictive.

Potentially more dangerous.

I leaned back against the counter. There was no way a trip to that taco place would be long enough for me to get my shit together. Now I knew what it was like to kiss her...

The memory would need to be burned out of my brain. I'd need someone to take a red-hot poker to it just so I'd be able to look at her and not want to do it again.

How was I meant to forget what it was like to have her body yielding to mine? To feel the rapid beat of her heart against her chest? To feel her gasp and shudder and touch me back?

Motherfucker—I'd just cursed myself. I'd cursed myself with the memory of Jamie Bell and her smartass mouth finally silenced.

Jesus, yes. I'd silenced that smart little mouth. That revelation didn't help.

Now, I'd want to kiss her every single time she opened it and sassed me.

How the fuck were we meant to work together now?

---

One hour later, Jamie slid into the garage with a paper bag with the logo of the taco place on. I slid out from beneath the car and met her gaze across the garage.

She lifted the bag lamely. "It's probably cold, but here. Your lunch."

"What about yours?" I got up and followed her to the staff area.

"I already ate. I ate there and ordered yours before I left." She set the bag on the countertop and turned on the coffee machine. "Is that a problem?"

I paused. "No. It's your lunch break. You can do what you like with it."

She flashed me a smile and grabbed her mug from the cupboard. The spluttering of the coffee machine and rustle of my lunch as I unwrapped it filled the need for conversation.

The awkwardness that hung between us was palpable. It was almost electric, hovering uncomfortably in mid-air. Waiting for one of us to address what had just happened.

I ate and watched as Jamie finished making her coffee. The strap of her dungarees kept sliding off her shoulder, and after pulling it back up three times, she made a "hmph" noise and pulled her arm out of the strap, leaving it to hang by her side.

I hid my laughter when she turned around.

"Something funny?" she asked, eyebrow quirked.

I shook my head. "Thinking about you in striped socks again," I answered.

I hadn't been, but now that I was...

"You know, the ones that go over your knees? They'd look great with those shorts." I paused. "And probably without them, too."

She blinked those wide, blue eyes at me, but there was no innocence or humor back in them. "Are you being an asshole to purposely stop me from asking you what the hell you were playing at earlier?"

"Even if I was, it clearly didn't work." I shoved the last bite of the taco into my mouth and crumpled up the paper. I tossed it toward the trash can and it bounced in off the side.

Jamie watched it fall in and then looked at me expectantly. She even cocked her hip and put her hand on it. "Well?"

"I'm sorry," I said around a mouthful of my second taco. "Was I meant to answer that?"

Her pursed lips said everything she didn't need to.

"Right." I wiped my mouth with my hand and set down my food. "Well, this might be fairly obvious, but I kissed you."

"No, stop, really?" she deadpanned, not missing a beat. "That's what that was? Well slap my ass and call me Sally, that was a new experience."

"I'm going to do it again if you keep up with that sarcastic bullshit."

She shoved her finger in my direction. "If you do that again, I'll rip your eyes out of their goddamn sockets."

"Have you ever kissed yourself, darlin'? It's a risk I'd be willing to take."

Her cheeks flushed. Embarrassment or anger? Who knew?

"You're insufferable, do you know that? You had no right to kiss me. I told you that you should have done it on Saturday, not there and then!"

"And you had every chance to push me away," I said dryly. "I didn't see you doing that while you grabbed onto my shirt and kissed me back."

"How could I push you away? You had me pinned to the truck!"

"I'm going to pin you to that wall and shut you

163

the fuck up in a minute."

"You dare!" Her eyes narrowed, and something flashed in them—something darker and more passionate. "You pin me to that wall and I'll pin your balls to a goddamn dartboard!"

I got up and rounded the coffee table, keeping my eyes firmly on hers. Another flush rose up her cheeks, and she clenched her fists as I got closer to her.

And closer.

Close enough to smell the coffee on her breath.

Close enough to smell the lingering perfume on her skin.

Close enough that she stepped back once, then twice, and then a third time.

Every time she stepped, so did I. I didn't reach for her or touch her. I invaded her personal space, and by the time she'd stopped walking, she'd pinned herself to the wall.

"Looks like I don't have to do anything except get close to you," I said in a low voice. "And you're the one who put your back against the wall, darlin'."

"You sneaky bastard," she muttered.

A smile tugged at one side of my mouth. I reached between us and cupped her chin, forcing her head back and her to meet my gaze.

I searched her eyes.

Anger and confusion were tainted with the honesty of how she was feeling.

With lust.

She could deny it, but she wanted me to kiss

her again, just as much as I wanted to kiss her.

I wanted to take her lips with mine right here, right now. Less rough. More softly—more deeply. Really explore her mouth with my tongue and see how far I could take her before she'd ask for more.

The thought made me smile wider.

She'd never ask for more. She'd never give in, no matter how much she'd want to.

She watched me. Almost expectantly, like she was waiting for it. She wasn't going to fight or push me away. She wanted it just like I did.

But it was a bad idea. One kiss was one kiss too many. I already wanted more than I could have from her.

Nobody told my body that.

Still gripping her chin, I leaned in and brushed my mouth over hers. Her lips parted, and I captured her lower lip between mine. Slowly, I grazed my teeth over her lip, dragging gently until I'd released it.

"Nice try," I whispered, my open eyes on her closed ones. "Maybe if you weren't so obvious, you'd have been able to convince me that you don't want me to kiss you."

Her eyes snapped open. "I hate you." She shoved me away and, grabbing her coffee, stormed out of the room into the workshop.

"You know what they say about hating someone," I called after her, stopping in the doorway.

She looked over her shoulder. "Don't worry. I

won't cross the fine line into loving you, asshole."

"I wasn't talking about that." I smirked. "I was going to tell you there's a fine line between hating someone and fucking them."

"Good thing you've got a spare hand, then, because that's the closest you're getting to fucking anything with your stunning personality." She slammed down the lid of a toolbox to punctuate her words. "Now, if you don't mind, I have work to do."

"And, if you don't mind," I reached over to grab a taco. "I'll eat my lunch and watch you."

She shot me a dark look. "You owe me twelve bucks."

"I'll pay you back." I smirked again.

Jamie simply glared at me before storming off to work.

God.

She was one hell of a firecracker, and why the fuck was that so hot?

# 16

## JAMIE

"He does it to piss me off, you know. It's bullshit. There's nothing he likes more than riling me up. It's like some fucked-up fucking foreplay, and there's nothing I can do, because he seems to have my damn manual. He can push all my buttons in all the right combinations. And my God, I'm trying, but one day, I'm going to flip my shit and he's going to come face to face with my temper." I sighed and sat right back. "I mean, what can I do? He kissed me when he didn't need to, and the worst part of it all is that if he kissed me now, I probably wouldn't push him away. It's so messed up. I'm so messed up. I hate his guts, but I can't stop wanting him, either. What am I supposed to do about this?"

My mom's cat, Barbie, blinked her liquid-amber eyes at me. "Merow."

"Yeah. Merow." I resumed my stroking of her back, and she purred once again. "Why am I even telling you? You're a cat. This isn't Disney. You're not going to suddenly start talking, are you? If only."

"Are you talking to the cat again?" Dad asked, joining me in the living room.

"Yes. She doesn't answer back. It's a nice change from work." I scratched Barbie under the chin, and her purr got louder. "That's right," I cooed. "You just listen and listen, don't you, Barbs? Good girl. You like that."

Dad looked at me as if I'd lost it.

I had. I'd lost it. And I didn't even care. There was no chance it—whatever it was—was coming back until these next two weeks were up.

"Still struggling at the garage?" He sat down in his armchair and picked up his glasses. He perched him on his nose and peered over at me. "Didn't you go out with him this weekend?"

"I didn't go out with him." I stilled my hands. "His grandfather tricked me into attending his great-aunt's birthday with him, and since you always taught me to respect my elders, I had to go."

"Merow." Barbie glared at me, protesting my lack of attention.

"All right, all right." I, once again, continued pleasing the queen of the household.

Dad side-eyed the cat. He never did like her. "Fine, sure. You were being respectful. If that's what the kids call it these days."

"I'm not a kid."

"You're sure acting like it."

"Only around Dex. And it's not my fault he

gets on my nerves. He knows just what to say and do to get under my skin." I huffed. "What am I supposed to do? Ignore him?"

Dad set his tablet down on his lap. "Yes, darling. That's exactly what you do. By all accounts, your relationship is based on a foundation of solid bickering and uncomfortable attraction."

"Please stop talking."

"And he knows how get your motor running, so to speak."

"Dad. No."

"Ignore him. Stop letting him get to you, and eventually, you'll reach a peaceful harmony."

"Okay, for a start." I held out one finger. "There's nothing peaceful about him. At all. Not even when he shuts his cakehole."

Barbie jumped onto the floor. Apparently, I was no longer interesting to her.

"And to continue," I went on, "bickering is how we cope with each other. Our so-called 'relationship' is built upon nothing but hatred and, fine, an uncomfortable attraction."

"Ah, the way all good relationships start," Mom said, walking in with Barbie in her arms.

The cat was a traitor. She didn't care who gave her attention, and she got it.

I stared at Mom as she sat down. "No, Mother, that is not the way all good relationships start. They start with a little bit of mutual respect and actually, oh, being able to tolerate being in the presence of the other person."

A smile curled her lips. "I saw you eating pizza

on your doorstep on Saturday."

Dad chuckled.

"No, no, that's not tolerance. All right, so it was, but it was after he hadn't been so...Dex...all night. He was actually likable for a few hours." Why was this hard for my parents to understand?

"I think you like each other a whole lot more than you think you do," Mom said, running her hand over Barbie's white fur. "But you're both so conditioned into hating each other because of the way you met that admitting it is akin to a death wish."

"I'd rather die," I admitted. "If I liked him, that was."

Dad chuckled again.

"Glad to see my misery is amusing to you, Dad." I huffed and folded my arms across my chest, staring at the TV.

"Your misery isn't amusing, Jamie. It's your stubbornness. You get that from your mother."

Mom snorted. "Gets it from me indeed. She gets it from you, honey, and that's the truth."

"Nope. Definitely you."

"Over my dead body."

I stood up. "While you two are being stubborn about being stubborn, I'm going to shower. Text me when dinner's ready, could you?"

I left while they were still arguing over who'd given me my stubborn streak.

The irony...

Rain beat down on the garage roof. It pitter-pattered against the window behind me and the metal doors to the repair shop. For the first time since I'd worked here, the doors were shut, meaning the fluorescent lights gave the area a horrible, bright haze that had already given me a headache.

I blew into my mug of soup, doing my best to ignore the way Charley peeked up from her coloring every few seconds. Dex had apparently been wrangled into babysitting again while Roxy had another interview.

Charley glanced up at me, staring for a second before looking away again.

I never appreciated how creepy kids were until right this second. I swear, the kid looked into my soul, and every time she did, she uncovered some deep, dark freaking secret.

I felt like I was in the middle of a damn horror movie.

She looked at me the way all the demon kids did before they killed you.

Would anyone hear my scream?

Sheesh.

Charley glanced up again, and I couldn't take it anymore.

"Do you need something?" I asked her.

She clutched her red pen tightly. "Are you the reason Uncle Dex was angry last night?"

All right. Wasn't expecting that.

"Uh...I don't know. Did he say I was?"

She pursed her lips. "He said something about

that...sucking woman."

Good to know she had more than one cuss word replacement.

"Oh. Uh, well, maybe?" It came out as more of a question than a reply. "I really don't know," I said honestly.

I mean, I probably was, but I couldn't explain why to a seven-year-old, could I?

Charley nodded and capped her pen. She dropped it back into the mug with a clink. "He moaned for ages until Pops told him to shut his beaver's butt."

"His beaver's butt?"

She looked side to side, then leaned forward and whispered conspiratorially, "His damn ass."

His damn...

Ha.

Ten points to Roxy. That was a good one.

I pointed at Charley and gave her a thumb up with a nod. "Got it. Did he shut up?"

She sighed with the attitude of a teen. "It's Uncle Dex. Do *you* think he shut up?"

I didn't even need to consider it. "Not a chance."

"It went on for *hours*. He said he'd fire her to keep his sanity if it didn't mean she'd win. Then Aunt Greta told him if he didn't pipe down and let her watch her show, she'd take a wrench and shove it—"

"Thank you, Charley," Dex drawled, joining us in the staff room. "That's enough about family game night."

"It wasn't family game night!" she exclaimed, sitting bolt upright. "It was you driving everyone insane night!"

I hid my smile behind my mug as I sipped my hot soup.

"Knew this was a bad idea," he muttered.

"Besides, I didn't even tell her the worst bit because I still want my ice cream you promised me if I didn't tell her."

"The worst bit?" I looked between them both. "It gets worse."

"For hi—"

"Shoop." Dex clapped his hands. "Shush, Charley."

"No, let her talk." I glared at him. "What have you been saying about me?"

"Something she shouldn't have been listening to in the first place," he ground out, turning his dark stare from her to me. "It was between me and Rox."

I put my mug on the table and stood up. "Well, now it's between you and me, so spit it out."

He said nothing, just continuing to glare at me.

I met his gaze beat for beat, intensity for intensity. I wasn't going to back down on this. Charley hadn't told me stuff I didn't already know. Well, mostly.

"Do I still get my ice cream?" she asked in a small voice.

Dex relaxed. "Yes. I promise. There's nothing booked in after lunch, so I'll take you, okay?"

"Okay," she answered, brightening and reaching for her pens again.

I stared at the side of Dex's head. He was deliberately focusing on her to ignore me, so I grabbed my mug and stormed out of the room. I didn't care if he followed me. As much as I wanted to know what he'd been saying, right now, I wanted to talk to him even less.

The only thing I could handle right now was being well away from him.

For the first time ever, I was glad when the phone rang.

I darted through to reception with my soup in hand, then grabbed the phone and answered. It was a standard request, so I booked it in, said goodbye, and hung up.

When I put the phone down, Dex was staring at me.

"What?" It came out harsher than I'd intended.

He hesitated. "I deserved that."

I glared at him. "Unless you're going to tell me what you said and apparently want to keep quiet or give me something to do, I don't care about what you have to say."

"It wasn't that bad. It's just Charley overexaggerating like kids do."

"If it's not that bad, there's no reason to keep it from me." I folded my arms. "Whatever. I don't care."

He raised an eyebrow as if to silently call me a liar—which I was—and leaned against the counter. "There's nothing booked in after lunch, and nothing booked this morning that I can't handle myself. You can take the day off if you want."

"In other words, you don't need me, so I can take my bad mood and go away."

"Now you're just putting words in my mouth."

"Well, they're arguably better than the ones you spew all by yourself."

His lips twitched into the tiniest of smiles. "Not many people can make me speechless, but you just did it."

"Yet, here you are, still speaking." I rolled my eyes and tucked my hair behind my ear. "If I can really go..."

"You can go." He held up his hands. "Preferably before you try to murder me."

"Cute. You think those thoughts are restrained just to today. I won't forget this." I wiggled my finger in his face, then hit him with one final glare before I stormed off toward the staff room.

Charley looked up when I clanged my mug into the sink. "Oh no, Jamie. Are you mad?"

I took a deep breath, turned, and smiled at her. I was, but not at her, and she didn't deserve to feel my anger just because her uncle was an ass.

"I'm fine," I reassured her. "I'm just going home because there's nothing to do."

She cocked her head to the side. "Not because Uncle Dex has been talking about you to my mom?"

"Absolutely not," I lied smoothly. "There's

nothing to do, that's all. There's no point me sitting around here for that, huh?"

"No, I suppose not." She capped her pen and looked at the ceiling thoughtfully. "You look sad."

"Maybe I'm a little mad," I finally gave in. "But not at you, okay?"

"Are you really going home because you're mad? Or are there really no cars?"

"Bit of both." There was no point lying to the kid. She was smart as hell. "But it's okay."

Slowly, she nodded, picking another pen out of her cup. "You should get ice cream with us. Ice cream makes everything better."

She wasn't lying.

"I don't think that's a good idea," I said softly.

"Why not?"

I paused. How the hell did you explain stuff like this to a kid? "Well, me and your Uncle Dex aren't friends right now, so I don't think ice cream would be very fun for you."

"Oh," she said in a small voice. "Okay. I understand."

"I'm sorry. Maybe another time?"

That made her brighten. "You promise?"

"Sure. I promise."

# 17

## DEX

Charley stared at me over the top of her chocolate sundae. Slowly, she dipped the spoon into the sauce and ice cream and put it in her mouth, the whole time keeping that devil-glare fixed on me.

If you've never had a seven-year-old stare at you as if you broke the head off her Barbie...Well, you're a luckier person than I am.

"Why are you staring at me like that?"

Charley's spoon clinked against the side of the sundae glass when she released it. Then, she sat back against the leather seats of the booth, arms folded across her chest.

I was in trouble.

With a kid.

Jesus.

"I asked Jamie to come to ice cream with us."

I knew where this was going.

"And she said no, because you made her mad."

She raised her light little eyebrows and gave me a

pointed look. "And I'm sad because I wanted her to have ice cream to make her happy again."

"Ice cream doesn't make people happy, Char."

"Neither do you, Uncle Dex."

That was... unexpected.

"What does that mean?"

"I think you're mean to Jamie." She stuck out her lip. "You fight with her all the time."

"Hey, she fights with me, too."

Charley sighed and leaned forward. "But we aren't talking about Jamie, Uncle Dex. We're talking about you."

She needed to stop listening to my sister.

"All right, I'll bite, little one. How am I so mean to her?" I sat back and moved my bowl to the side so I could see her properly.

She shifted in her seat, resting her hands on the table like a newsreader.

I felt like I was back in high school and getting read the riot act from the principal...except this principal was about three-feet-tall.

"You're mean to her all the time. You don't even want her to work in the garage because I heard you say that to Pops. I don't think you want to be friends with her." Her eyes widened in earnest. "And I don't like it when you're mean to her because I think she's really nice. And, quite frankly, I've had enough of your banana split."

*Ahh.* Words Pops said to Aunt Greta just last night at dinner...except it wasn't banana split.

This kid picked way too much up.

Not to mention, she did kind of have a point.

"All right. I think you're right. Not totally right, but a little bit right." I pinched my finger and thumb together. "And I didn't want her to work in the garage when she started, but now, she's pretty good, and I'm okay with it." Kind of.

She sighed. "Well, you could show it."

Yep. I needed words with my sister.

"How would I do that?"

Charley pursed her lips into a fish-mouth shape and tapped them with her finger, staring off into the distance.

I waited.

"Mommy says that when you're mean to someone, you should say sorry. So you should say sorry to Jamie for being mean to her."

"That sounds like a good plan."

"Right now."

I did a double-take. "Right now? As in right this second?"

Charley nodded firmly. "I want to make sure you say sorry properly."

"Are you an expert in saying sorry?"

She rolled her eyes. "It's not *my* fault Faith keeps getting in my way and tripping over my feet at school."

I bit the inside of my cheek to stop myself laughing. "All right, then, apology expert. Let's go."

She jumped out of her seat. "We need ice cream first."

"We do?"

"Duh. She didn't get any because you were

mean. So now you have to take her some."

Sweet baby Jesus...

---

"Do you remember what to say?" Charley asked from the back seat.

"I'm capable of crafting a basic apology," I replied. "Is that ice cream still frozen?"

She nodded. "Mostly."

Mostly was good enough.

This whole exercise would be a fiasco. I didn't even know if she was home, for fuck's sake. Or alone.

Fuck, if she wasn't alone, I'd never live this down.

Thankfully, when I pulled up outside her house next to her Mustang, there were no other cars. Hopefully that meant she was alone.

"Remember," I said to Charley as I opened the back door. "You're just here for the ice cream, okay?"

She nodded, holding the plastic sundae glass like it was made of pure gold.

I knocked on the front door.

"I got it!" came from inside.

I knew that voice, and it wasn't Jamie's.

Shit.

The door swung open, revealing Haley wearing gym clothes with her hair in a messy bun on top of her head. She had on no makeup, but that didn't stop her gaze being any less chilling.

"What," she said slowly, "The hell do you want?"

Charley leaned against my leg.

"I'm just here to apologize," I told her. "Is Jamie here?"

Haley folded her arms. "I doubt she wants to speak to you right now."

"That wasn't my question."

"She just printed your Facebook profile picture, taped it to a punching bag, and went to town on your face. I don't care what your question is."

That was brutal.

"Who is it?" Jamie walked into view of the front door. Like Haley, she had on no makeup, but her unruly hair hung in wet curls over her shoulders as she towel-dried it, and she was wearing her usual uniform of a tank top and denim shorts.

Unlike Haley, she didn't look at me like I needed to drop dead on the spot.

"Oh. Do I need to come back to work? You could have called—"

"No, no. The garage is closed. I just wanted to talk to you." I did my best to ignore Haley's death stare.

Charley held out the sundae tub. "I brought you ice cream. Because you were sad."

Jamie smiled, throwing the towel to the side. "Do you know what? Ice cream is just what I wanted right now, Charley. Thank you so much." She nudged Haley out of the way and bent down to take the ice cream.

Charley beamed with delight at her.

Jamie kissed her cheek, then stood back up, holding the ice cream. "What did you want?"

"Actually," I said, glancing at a still-glaring Haley, "Do you mind if I come back? I'd prefer to talk to you in private."

Charley sighed.

Jamie glanced at Haley, too. "No, that's fine. I have to take Haley home, so... do you want to come back in half an hour?"

"Sure. I'll see you then. C'mon, Charley. Aunt Greta was baking this morning." I steered her away from the door before she could start something I wasn't prepared to finish in front of Haley.

When we were in the car, Charley groaned. "You didn't do it."

I met her eyes in the rearview mirror. "I promise I will when I come back. Her friend doesn't like me much."

"She did look a bit mean," she agreed. "Is she going home now?"

"Yeah, she is." I reversed and turned to go down the long driveway. "That's why I'm coming back."

"Do you promise you'll apologize?"

"Cross my heart, kid. Cross my heart."

# 18

## JAMIE

"He's a jerk."

That was the third time Haley had said that in the last two minutes. "I know that," I said, turning onto her street. "Believe me, I know better than anyone what he is, but he's still my boss."

"You screamed that you were going to quit when you were laying into the punching bag."

"It was therapeutic." I pulled up outside her apartment. "I'm not really going to quit. If I quit, he wins."

"Oh, Jesus. It was funny at first, but now?" Haley turned and looked at me. "Not anymore, James. This battle thing you've got going on is just weird. How can he prove you're not good enough? What if he fires you anyway?"

"Haley..."

"That's all the things you just screamed at his photo taped to a punching bag," she said dryly.

"You don't want to work there. You're there to prove a point."

That was the thing.

A part of me did want to work there... even if he was a jerk, because I knew—*knew*—he was only like that with me. And only at work.

And that didn't make him a bad person. After all, I'd seen the other side of him this past weekend at his aunt's party. And that was nothing like the Dex I saw at work all the time.

We set each other off. Alone, he was gasoline and I was a lit match. Together, we were a raging inferno.

"I don't know why you're going to talk to him. I don't think his apology will be up to much."

I raised a brow. "He told you he was there to apologize?"

"God knows what for. He's probably the kind of person who walks into a chair and blames it for being in the way."

"That's no different to apologizing to one."

"Of course it is. For one, you're taking the blame."

"Whatever. I have to get back. Should I call you later, or am I just going to make you angry?"

"Probably the latter one. If my curiosity gets the better of me, I'll text you."

I smirked. "You mean when it does."

She flipped me the bird over her shoulder and got out of the car. I watched her walk into her house, then pulled away from the curb.

My mind whirred at a million miles an hour.

He was going to apologize? For the obvious, or for a whole lot more?

He wasn't the only one who had to apologize. Even though I hadn't done anything wrong, my temper had definitely reached a point of almost no return. If Charley hadn't been there, I might have lost it entirely.

And, really, was it my business if he'd been talking about me? If Charley hadn't have mentioned it, I'd never have known. Some things weren't worth knowing about, and that was one of them.

I'd be lying if I said I didn't want to know what he'd said. Of course I did. I human, and I was curious.

I got home a few minutes later—perks of a small town—and waited in my car for a couple of minutes. What had I been thinking when I asked him to come here? I didn't want him in my house. That was way too personal.

The rumble of his truck came from behind, and any fleeting thought I'd had about calling him to meet somewhere disappeared.

Damn it.

I steeled myself and got out of my car, clutching my keys in one hand and my phone in the other. "Hey," I said when Dex caught up with me at the front door.

"Hey. Sorry—I know this is awkward."

"No, it's fine. Come in." I walked inside and tossed my keys into the bowl on the side table. My phone stayed firmly with me as I moved through to the kitchen door. "You can take a seat. I just need to do some laundry."

I darted into the kitchen and dragged the basket across the floor. It tipped up on its side, and instead of sighing, I slowly separated the whites from the colors and the darks.

All right, I was killing time. As much as I wanted to hear what Dex was going to apologize for, I didn't want to be alone with him in my house.

Because I wasn't even angry anymore. A part of me didn't even care that he'd been talking about me because I had been about him. That was human nature—how else were you supposed to figure stuff out? Sometimes you needed a sounding board, and if the thing you needed to sound off on was a person...

Well.

The wall wouldn't be very helpful, would it? It wasn't a police investigation with pictures and goddamn memo cards.

I set the load going and hovered in the doorway. "Can I get you a drink?"

"Nah, I'm good." He paused, looking back at me. "You don't need to look at me like I'm gonna bite you, darlin'. I only do that on request."

I pursed my lips and sat on the arm of the sofa. "Haley said you were here to apologize. Was that it? It sucked."

His lips pulled into a smile. "It was an unspoken offer."

I stared at him flatly. "You do that when you're

uncomfortable. Have you noticed?"

"No, but I probably will now."

"You're welcome."

"You get really snarky when you're uncomfortable. Have you noticed that?"

I raised an eyebrow. "Yes. It's called self-preservation. And this is not an apology."

Dex rubbed his hand down his face. "You're right. Shit. You put me all out of fucking sorts all the damn time."

Was that a compliment?

Nah. It was a frustration. Maybe a weird mix of both.

"Um, okay." I clasped my hands in my lap and waited for him to speak more.

"I wanted to say I'm sorry for this morning." He leaned back, one arm over the back cushions.

Our eyes met, and there was no deception. He really meant it.

"Charley laid into me over lunch, as much as I hate admitting a seven-year-old kicked my ass."

I looked down and smiled.

"In her words, I'm "mean" to you. And...she's kinda right. I am. And there's no excuse for the way I speak to you sometimes, so I'm sorry."

I peered back up at him and pushed my now-dry, wildly curly hair behind my ear. It popped right back out again. "Well, thank you. I appreciate the apology."

Dex grinned—a real, genuine smile that made his eyes light up. Made him look pretty damn handsome, too. "I promise I'll do better to be nice to you." He got up and walked to the door.

"Dex, wait." I followed him and caught him opening the front door. I slid past him and clicked it shut.

He looked at me quizzically. "Yeah, I know I didn't say anything wrong this time..."

"I'm sorry, too." I threw the words out before I could change my mind. "I...don't exactly make it easy for us to get along."

He tilted his head to the side, pinning me with his gaze.

I rolled my shoulders awkwardly, holding my hair back from my face. "So...you're not the only one who could try harder or watch what they say. If you're willing to try, then I am, too."

"Look at that," he muttered through a smile. "The sassy one has a heart under there."

"See, that." I pointed at him and shook my head.

He laughed. "I'm kidding. Don't sweat it, Jamie. We're just different people and we clash."

"Actually... We're not that different." I fiddled with the hem of my shirt, glancing down for a second. "We're both pretty stubborn—"

"I take offense to that."

"—Which is the first sign of stubbornness," I continued. "We're pretty headstrong and determined, and with this whole set up... I mean, it doesn't help that only one of us can be right, and that's not going to be you."

"This apology went downhill real quick." His lips twitched as he fought laughter.

I touched my fingers to my mouth. "The best apologies are honest ones."

"Continue." He laughed.

"We're just really similar, and that leads to personality clashes. That's all." I smiled and dropped my hand back to play with my fraying hem. "Maybe now that we've recognized it, we'll be able to be friends."

Dex's tongue slipped out and ran over his lips. I didn't mean to look, but it was such a deliberate move I couldn't help it.

Heat flashed in his eyes when I met his gaze.

"In the nicest possible way, we're never gonna be friends, Jamie," he said in a low voice.

I swallowed. "We're not?"

"Nope."

"Why not?"

He looked me dead in the eye and said, "Because friends don't want to fuck their friends."

I inhaled sharply.

"See?" His lips twitched. "We can't be friends, darlin'. There are a lot of things friends do, but that ain't one of them in my experience."

"Well, you obviously haven't had very good friends." I slapped my hand over my mouth.

His eyebrows shot up. "You wanna be friends knowing I want to fuck the living daylights out of you?"

My mouth opened and closed a few times, but all I did was end up clearing my throat and moving back closer to the front door.

Well.

That was short and to the point.

"Well, that—that might change things a little." I swallowed. Hard.

Dex stepped toward me and pinged one of my unruly curls. "Of course it does. It makes a huge difference. Because now, you won't be able to take one of my comments as a joke. Now, you won't be able to have a casual taco lunch with me without wondering if I'm thinking about screwing you over the table."

This escalated quickly.

So did my heartbeat.

"And that's the reason I'm an ass to you, Jamie. Not because I don't like you. I don't *want* to like you, and the more I push you away, the more likely it is that I'll never have to live with the memory of what it's like to be lying over you, stark naked, with my cock buried inside you while you moan my name."

Oh, Jesus.

How the hell did I reply to that?

"What does it matter?" I lifted my chin, even though all I wanted to do was run. "If we're not going to be friends, what does it matter if you do fuck me?"

"Because we work together." He slid his fingers down my jaw and cupped my chin. His thumb brushed across the curve of my lower lip, and I let out a shuddery breath. "And you don't really want that, do you? You want to be friends."

"You think you can tell me you know what I want?"

He leaned in, a smile playing on his lips. "Three hours ago, you didn't want to be anywhere near me. Now, you want to be as close to me as two people can get? Three hours ago, darlin', you didn't want to be in the same building as me. Now you're trying to tell me you want, what? My tongue? My fingers? My cock? All inside you? I don't believe you."

My stomach clenched, and I ignored the way goosebumps rose across my skin.

He ghosted his thumb over my lower lip once more, this time lightly tugging it down. His gazed flitted from my mouth to my eyes, hinting at indecision, at his inability to decide whether or not I was serious.

And right now?

I was.

I wanted to be friends, but if that would never happen, by his own admission, then what was the point? It was going to be awkward tomorrow no matter what happened.

Dex stepped back and adjusted his pants.

I glanced down and looked away straight away when I saw his cock obviously pushing against his jeans. The outline was clear, and hell, if I had another dirty dream about him because of this...

"I'll see you tomorrow, darlin'." He put his hand on the door handle, which was my cue to move.

I did. Like a squirrel that had been kicked.

His eyes sparkled as he laughed.

He left, leaving me with the sound of his

laughter and the rapid beating of my own heart.

# 19

## JAMIE

He was fucking with me.

That had to be the explanation. There was no way he really felt the way that he did. No, not a chance. If he did, he wouldn't have walked away, right?

That's what I was telling myself. There's no way he would say that and not act on it. Not after the way he'd kissed me—both times. So very different, but both so very real.

No, him walking away went against everything I knew about him. Was he bluffing, or was he really making a smart choice not to take this attraction further?

Was the even the smart choice? He admitted to pushing away, which meant that, in about ten days, I'd be out of my job.

I could accept that. Realistically, this wouldn't work long term. I wasn't naïve enough to believe that it would. I'd still do my best to prove him wrong, though. Even if it was only to make him admit he was wrong.

I was pretty sure he already knew that, though.

Of course, none of that explained why I'd gone for the denim skirt over the shorts this morning.

That was purely to see if he'd been bluffing.

Hey—my parents always said I'd been a limit-tester as a child. Apparently, it was a trait I'd retained well into adulthood.

I pulled up outside the garage. It was starting to lightly rain again, so I pulled the hood of my sweatshirt over my head, grabbed my things, and ran to the safety of the garage. I locked the car when I was in the dry.

"Hey," Dex called from under a car.

"Hey. It's raining. I'm closing the doors."

He slid out. "I'll get the other."

He joined me at the doors and slid the first one down. I dumped my purse and handled the second one. Dex locked them both, then turned to me with a smile as rain pelted against the metal. "Just in time."

"No kidding." I picked up my purse and walked into the staff room. "Is it busy today?"

Dex leaned against the doorway. "Not really. It's a lot of sitting around and hoping Mr. Daniels hasn't killed his fucking battery again."

"Don't. Do not jinx that."

"Jinx is bullshit."

"Nope. My dad said that once and an hour later..."

Dex slapped his hand against his forehead.

"Shit. All right—forget I said it."

I hit the button on the coffee machine and held out my hands. "I can, but the universe might not."

"Damn it." He swiped the mug of coffee out from under the machine.

"What the hell?" I threw my arms in the air and made a swipe for it.

He jerked back and splattered it all over the floor. "Damn it, Jamie, now you made me spill the coffee."

"I made you? You spilled it! You're the one who stole *my* coffee!"

"It's just coffee!"

My eyebrows shot up, and he froze in place.

"Okay," he said slowly. "Okay, darlin', let's take a deep breath and sit down." He carefully put the now half-full mug down on the counter and turned to me, gripping my shoulders. He sat me down on the sofa with an earnest look. "Let me make you a coffee."

I stared at him as he moved to the coffee machine and began the process of making me a new mug. I was mildly annoyed, but only because, once again, I'd woken up late and not had coffee before I'd gotten here. I'd had enough of a mind to shower and dress mildly inappropriately, but not to get coffee.

Hey, I had priorities, and I couldn't get dressed here in the garage, could I?

"Here." Dex carefully handed me another cup of coffee.

I took it from him and sipped, keeping my eyes on him. He'd made it exactly the way I liked it, down to the right amount of cream.

"Thank you," I said quietly, resting the mug on the arm of the sofa.

"Remind me never to steal your coffee again." He grabbed a second mug and put it beneath the machine.

"I'll write it on a Post-It and stick it to that cupboard." I pointed to the one right above the coffee machine.

His laughter echoed through the room. "I'll set an eight a.m. reminder on my phone just in case it falls down."

"There we go. It was a shaky start, but look at us, getting along and all that shit."

Dex met my eyes.

I grinned over the rim of my mug.

His smile slowly grew until it matched mine. "Well, fuck. We did it. We got along."

"Only just. Don't get cocky."

"I don't know how to be anything but cocky with you, Jamie."

"Is that literally or metaphorically?"

He poured some cream into his coffee. Added sugar. Stirred. Tapped the spoon against the rim. Dropped the spoon into the sink. Grabbed the spoon.

Turned to me.

Grinned.

"Now, now," he said in a low voice. "Why would I clarify that?"

Why, indeed?

"Just asking." I sipped the coffee. "What's on the schedule for me today?"

"Basics. You've got an M.O.T, service, and tire change. Coming in in an hour."

"You spoil me." I swung my feet up onto the sofa and stretched my legs out. I pulled a cushion onto my lap to rest my coffee on and looked back at him. "Is that all?"

He leaned back, cradling his cup against his muscular chest. "That's all, darlin'. You sit there and chill out until it comes in."

"You're laying this friendship thing on a little thick."

"Friendship is still off the card, but I was gonna buy you tacos for lunch. Never mind." He walked past me.

"Whoa, whoa, whoa!" I sat up, only just avoiding spilling my coffee. "Come back right now."

He turned in the doorway, looking at me over his shoulder.

His five o'clock shadow was a little darker today.

"Yeah, darlin'?"

"You said something about buying me tacos? I'm all about that kind of not-friends."

Blue eyes looked me up and down. "You're all about the food, aren't you?"

"You caught me." I settled back down into the cushions. "I'll even go buy it if you pay. How's that for a compromise?"

Dex blinked at me. "All right, but it's fucking weird."

He wasn't lying.

# 20

## DEX

I pulled into the parking lot, the smell of tacos emanating from the passenger seat. I have no idea how I got roped into doing the lunch trip. She said she would if I paid, but obviously, she changed her mind.

Which was exactly how I'd ended up getting lost on my way to the taco place.

Not that I was going to tell her that

Fuck knows I'd kept enough from her.

Like how badly I'd wanted to slam her against the door and fuck her to death after she'd challenged me yesterday. It'd taken everything I had not to give in and do it. Not do the thing I wanted that I knew she didn't.

She was saying it because of me. I wasn't blind and I wasn't stupid.

Sure, I'd felt the way she'd responded when I kissed her, but fucking her was a whole other ball game.

I could forget kissing her.

Maybe.

I definitely would not forget fucking her.

And if I did it, I wanted it to be more than just an itch I needed to scratch. I wanted to fuck her because I needed to—something more than a meaningless act.

Not that anything with her could ever be classified as meaningless.

Motherfucker, I wouldn't forget a damn thing about the woman who was slowly worming her way under my skin.

Slowly.

Who was I kidding?

She was six-inches deep.

I opened the garage door.

A scream sounded.

I shouted.

Jamie staggered backward, her hand on her chest until she was back against my half-repaired Dodge.

"Fuck me dead, Dex! Would you knock next time?" she shouted, rubbing her head. "You scared the hell out of me and I banged my head on the hood of that goddamn car!"

I burst out laughing, hesitating for only a second. "You want a bell on my neck, darlin'? Should I announce myself?"

She paused, screwdriver in hand. "Yes, actually. A bell would work fine, thank you."

"I have lunch." I held up the bag of tacos.

"That's the nicest thing you've ever said to me." She walked into the staff room, and the sound of the tap running filled the air.

I joined her. "Well, we made a deal, and this is me trying to stick to it."

"Food is the way to my heart," she said, grabbing a towel to dry her hands. "And tacos are the fastest path."

"As long as they're a fast-track past your sarcasm, I'll buy you tacos every day."

She clutched her hand to her chest. "Excuse me. I need a moment to swoon."

I laughed and laid them out on the table. "Swoon quickly, or they'll get cold. They're already halfway there."

She moved quicker than I'd ever seen her. Throwing herself on the sofa next to me, she bounced and grabbed a wrapped taco.

I blinked at her. "This is scary."

"What? Did my makeup run?"

"No. You willingly sitting next to me." I paused. "And the fact you're wearing the world's largest hoodie."

She looked down. "Oh. I'm preserving my dignity."

"You're preserving your dignity." Why did I want to know more about that? And, more to the point, what was she preserving it from? "I'm not going to ask."

I grabbed my own taco and unwrapped it before I did ask. I was curious. Was she not wearing anything under it? Was it like in those stupid movies where women showed up in nothing but lingerie and a trench coat?

I glanced at her legs.

Nope. No sign of lingerie there.

Damn. There went those hopes.

She laughed and covered her mouth with her hand so she didn't spit out her food. "Stop staring at my legs."

"I can't help it."

She eyed me. "I couldn't find any shorts this morning so I had to improvise."

"Jesus, Jamie, if you tell me you're not wearing anything under there..."

"Oh my God!" She laughed again. "I'm not naked underneath this sweater, Dex. Holy hell. I'm wearing a skirt instead of shorts and, well, the sweater is longer than the skirt."

Slowly, I chewed what was in my mouth. "You got no pants at home?"

"None that make my legs look as good as shorts do." She shrugged, grinned, and licked some taco sauce from the corner of her mouth.

"Yeah, 'cause that's how you decide what to wear for work. I ask myself every morning if my ass looks good in my jeans."

"It doesn't. Not in those."

I itched the side of my nose. "Your honesty is cutting."

"I'm just saying, I've seen your ass look better in worse pants."

"All I'm hearing is that you've been looking at my ass." I smirked.

"Look, I like a good ass as much as the next girl. Your ass is the best part about you."

She was totally honest as she said it, too.

I shook my head and got up to get a bottle of water from the fridge. "I know what you're doing."

"What?" She looked at me, blue eyes wide and innocent. "What am I doing?"

I tossed her a bottle and shut the door. "I don't need to say it because you know. You're a shit ass liar, darlin'."

Jamie's mouth formed a tiny 'o'. "I have no idea what you mean."

I eyed her before sitting back down. "Mhmm."

Her lips twitched, but she dipped her head and turned away before I could see how wide the smile got.

*She was playing me.*

And it was working, because I wanted to know more about that skirt.

Shit.

---

I put down the phone and walked back into the garage. After getting rid of one car, taking another, and two phone calls, I was out of tolerance for people. Which was exactly why I needed someone to do reception for me. I could do cars all day—people?

That was another story.

Jamie was sitting on the countertop at the side of the workshop. Her bare legs swung back and forth, and as I cast my gaze up and over them, there was one difference.

She'd taken off that damn sweater.

And the skirt was as short as it looked. At least, the way it rode up her thighs made it look like that way.

Shit.

I cleared my throat.

She glanced up from her phone. "Yes? Do you need me?"

Oh, shit.

"No. I was just..." I coughed.

She half-smiled.

"You weren't kidding about that skirt." My eyes wandered to her legs once more.

"My eyes are up here, Romeo."

"I know, but your legs are down here, darlin'."

She sighed and jumped off the counter. She tugged down the skirt, but it really didn't do much. "I wear shorts this short literally every day."

I hovered there a little longer before I brought my gaze back up to meet hers. "And I look at your legs literally every day. Not this obviously, but it still happens."

Jamie rolled her eyes and put her phone down. "We just managed a whole conversation without arguing."

"Mhmm." I turned away from her and discreetly adjusted my pants.

We might have managed it without arguing, but we didn't manage it without me thinking about how pointless the presence of that skirt was.

How easy it'd be to hike it up over her hips...

"I saw that!" Jamie called.

"Dunno what you're talking about!" I shouted right back.

"An earthquake is more discreet than your ability to adjust your pants, Dexter Ryne."

I groaned and turned around. "What do you expect me to do? I tell you yesterday I'd love to fuck you, and now you show up to *work* looking like that."

She held out her hands, the picture of innocence. "My shorts are all wet."

"If I had less restraint, your panties would be wet."

Pointedly, Jamie looked at my cock. "Oh, yes. Look at that restraint."

"It's inside my pants and not you. That is restraint."

She looked back up with a withering look. "Whose fault is that?" She raised her eyebrows quickly before turning and going to the six-foot-tall toolbox.

I watched as she opened a drawer and pulled out a wrench.

And it hit me.

I leaned against my Dodge and folded my arms, studying her for a moment. Her white tank top hugged her entire body perfectly, and the frayed hem of the skirt barely crept two inches beneath her ass.

"Wet shorts, huh?" I asked.

"Yep." She got down on her knees, flashing the

bright-red panties she was wearing.

*Motherfucker.*

"Nothing to do with the conversation we had yesterday, then?"

"The one where you said you wanted to fuck me then left?" She glanced over her shoulder with one eyebrow raised. "That one?"

"That one," I confirmed.

"Nope. Nothing at all. Wet shorts. I told you."

"You're the worst liar in the history of liars." I pushed off the wall and dropped my arms. "I've seen you wear at least five different pairs of shorts since you started working here. There's no way they're all wet."

"You took notice of my shorts?"

"Yeah. I stare at your legs a whole lot." I stopped next to her, grabbed her wrist, and pulled her up to standing.

She bit the inside of her cheek. "I forgot to do laundry."

"You did it yesterday while I was there."

"I didn't pull it out the washer." Her cheeks flooded bright pink.

"You're adorable when you lie. Or, rather, when you try to." I pulled her closer to me. "I think you wore that skirt on purpose because otherwise, you wouldn't have just flashed me your underwear."

Jamie wrangled her wrist from my hand and walked backward, only just avoiding tripping over a wire on the floor. "I swear, I have no idea what you're talking about."

"I think you wore it because you're trying to prove a point, except I don't know what that point is." I met her step-for-step, almost stalking her until she almost had her back against the tall toolbox.

Her tongue darted out over her lips. "You're losing me, Dex."

I closed the distance until she was flat against the front of the box.

"Watch it. I have a weapon." She held up the wrench.

With a smirk, I closed my hand around it and pulled it from her grip. It clattered to the floor, bouncing a few times before settling against a stack of tires.

"I don't have a weapon," she said, looking at her empty hand. "This is workplace harassment."

"Your skirt is workplace harassment. Admit you wore it on purpose and I might—*might*—leave you alone."

She swallowed, tilting her head up. "Fine. I admit it. I own about twenty pairs of denim shorts. I wore it on purpose."

"Because you're annoyed that you offered yourself to me on a silver platter and I threw you off the table?"

She met my eyes, and with more than a hint of amusement in them, said, "No. I thought it would be fun to see how you coped knowing you can look, but you decided not to touch."

I gripped the top of the toolbox and dipped my head. "I reserve the right to change my mind at any point."

Her tongue flicked out and wet her lips once more. "I don't think you do."

"What would you do if I touched you right now?"

"Right now? Push you away."

"Really? If I tucked your hair behind your ear and kissed your neck? What if I ran my fingertips up your thigh and gripped your ass? Would you push me away then?"

"I mean..." She paused. "I guess." She paused again. "Yes."

"You don't sound so certain there, darlin'."

"I'm not," she breathed.

I took my chance.

I dipped my head, cupped the back of her neck, and I fucking kissed her.

She grabbed my shirt, pulling me close to her, and flicked her tongue against my lower lip. A bolt of desire shot through me at that tiny movement, and I flattened my body against hers, pushing her right against the toolbox.

She squeaked. "Ouch. Drawers!"

I laughed, pulling her away from it, and swept her around the side of it instead. The metal clanged as her back went into it, and she bit her lip to stop herself grinning as I boxed her against it.

"Still unsure?" I asked.

She nodded.

So I kissed her again.

# 21

## JAMIE

His thumbs were rough against my cheeks as he cupped my face. I slid my hands up his body between us to do the same to his neck and pushed myself against him.

I knew this was beyond the line, and I didn't care. He'd crossed it yesterday when he'd said what he had, and yes, I had worn this skirt deliberately. I didn't even care.

I wanted to be friends.

If he didn't want that, I'd show him what he did want.

*Me.*

Dex flattened me against the side of the toolbox. His tongue battled against mine as his fingers slid into my ponytail and pulled out the hair tie. It fell somewhere to the floor, and I whimpered at the loss of today's hair restraint.

His chuckle against my lips sent shivers over my skin. I gripped him even tighter, and he dropped one hand to my bare thigh. His cock was hard against me, and my heart was beating crazy fast, but that didn't take away the sensation of his roughened fingertips gliding up my thigh.

Goosebumps.

I was covered in goosebumps. They trickled up and down my skin, sending shivers across me as they did so.

But there was just Dex. His tongue against mine, his fingers probing my skin. My fingers digging into his neck, the feel of his tiny stubble rubbing against my chin.

He grabbed my thighs and lifted me. I gasped, gripping the sides of the toolbox as he hooked my legs over his hips and grabbed my ass. My arms wound around his neck, and the kiss deepened to the point I could barely breathe.

I felt him everywhere. All over me. He danced across my skin and he pumped through my veins.

Like a drug, but better.

Addictive, just as wrong, but still so much better.

My hips pushed against his. My clit rubbed his hard cock, and his deft thumbs hiked my skirt up over my hips.

I didn't care. The adrenaline that was pounding through me only served to heighten my desire—the lust wound through my body tighter and harder than I'd ever felt it, and I knew, this time, it wouldn't end at a kiss.

I'd pushed him far enough.

I needed this.

I didn't know why. It was something—a

catalyst, a game-changer, I didn't know, but it was significant. Having sex with this man would change something about our relationship, and that was all I knew.

How we felt about each other—hatred, frustration, anger—it would all change after this.

I was scared, but I wanted him more than I feared what would happen next.

I don't know how it happened. I don't know how I went from hating him to wanting him, but it was what it was.

It was fucked up, but still.

Dex gripped my ass tighter and pulled his mouth back from mine, but only by an inch. "Jamie..."

"Um...Is now where I tell you there's a condom in my pocket?"

He froze. "Yes, but I wasn't expecting that."

I smacked my lips together. "There's a condom in my front left pocket."

"You were expecting this, weren't you?"

"No?" I offered the answer with a sweet smile.

Dex stared at me. He didn't say anything as he kissed me again. His fingers were inside my pocket in a second, and I felt him dig for the condom.

"Are you sure?" he murmured against my lips.

"No, I put the condom there to change my mind."

"You're hot when you're sassy."

"You're annoying when you don't get the hell on with it."

He groaned and unbuttoned his jeans. I watched as he hooked his thumbs under both his jeans and boxers waistband and pushed them down. They only went

to his knees, but they only needed to go that far.

He wrapped his hand around his long, hard cock. His eyes were on mine the whole time—all the seconds I wasn't looking at his cock, that was.

I peered up. He was smirking, and I couldn't even be mad. I felt no shame in the fact I was staring at him holding his cock.

If I felt shame for that, I had to feel it that I had my skirt up over my hips and hadn't tried to pull it down.

Dex ripped open the condom packet and pulled it out. I watched as he rolled it on and turned his attention back to me.

My lips were dry.

Apprehension tightened my muscles. It wasn't too late to back out, but was that really what I wanted to do?

No.

His eyes bore into mine as he closed the distance between us and picked me up once again. One of my arms wrapped around his neck and my lips found his as I stretched between us and guided his cock toward my wet pussy.

He lowered my hips slowly until he was inside me and I was gasping into his mouth. He groaned, gripping my ass tighter as he began to slowly thrust back and forth.

I grasped at his shoulders as he picked up the pace. Our kisses became a mixture of moans and gasps and tongue, and my skin became slick as pleasure snaked its way through my body.

My muscles tensed. My heart pounded. My adrenaline ran through me until I felt hotter than I'd ever been.

Dex's fingers probed my ass cheeks, and he held me against the side of the toolbox so firmly that my skin stuck to the metal.

I didn't care.

I wanted to go over the edge.

I wanted him to take me there.

I moaned against his lips, and he smiled, right before he grazed his teeth over my lower lip and kissed me hard.

He fucked me just as deep as he kissed me.

Hot and sweaty and crazy, we moved together in sync as my muscles clenched around him. My orgasm shot through me, and I cried out through the shiver that wracked my body.

I pressed my face against his shoulder. He kept moving until he groaned and stilled, holding my hips right against his. His breath was hot across my skin as we both took deep breaths to calm down.

"Good thing this box doesn't have wheels," Dex murmured against my skin.

I laughed as he gently pulled out of me and eased my legs down until my toes touched the garage floor. My legs were shaky, but being back against the toolbox helped me stay steady.

"There goes the friendship thing." Dex laughed to himself as he rolled off the condom.

"You're the one who put that off the table," I reminded him, shimmying my skirt down over my hips.

Ugh. Now it was gross there.

I pushed off the toolbox and on shaky legs, ran toward the bathroom.

"What are you doing?"

I glanced over my shoulder at a smirking Dex. "Have you ever had cum drip down your leg?"

He opened his mouth then closed it again. "Nope. Can't say I ever have."

I shot him a pointed look and slammed the door behind me. I put the toilet seat down and sat down, pulling a bunch of tissue from the holder.

Then, I just sat there.

Sat and stared at the door.

I'd just had sex with Dex.

Jesus, it rhymed.

Why was that my first thought? That sex rhymed with Dex?

What was wrong with me?

Oh, God.

I'd just had sex with Dex.

Against a goddamn toolbox.

That was a new one...

# 22

## DEX

I closed the drawer of the standing toolbox and leaned against it. I could hear Jamie laughing in reception with another woman, yet back here, I felt like I was burning up.

I rested my forehead against the cool metal of the box and let out a long sigh. I couldn't believe I'd given into her games. I couldn't believe I'd not been able to resist her. That I hadn't been strong enough to keep myself to myself.

That I'd crossed the fucking line. Crossed it into fucking torture, because now I knew what it was like. What it was like to have her nails digging into my skin and feel the vibrating of her moans against my lips.

What it was like to hear her as she let go of everything and was fully in the moment.

Fucking hell. How were we supposed to work together now? I knew I'd fucked up the moment I'd told her how bad I wanted her, but I never thought she'd actually push my buttons and do something about me turning her down.

This was why I'd turned her down.

Because I knew once wouldn't be enough.

I knew I'd want her again.

Gripping hold of her ass while I fucked her had been like a drug. I wanted the hit again. I wanted to feel the way I had when she'd gripped me as if her life depended on it.

I'd never be able to look at her the same way ever again. She was no longer the sarcastic, over-confident woman who'd walked into the garage and challenged me to prove me wrong.

She was something more—something wilder. Something more intriguing.

The door to reception opened, and the sound of Jamie humming filled the air. I didn't recognize the tune, and I didn't know what to say to her.

We'd barely spoken since she'd run off to the bathroom and did some so-called cleaning up. Cleaning up that had taken her twenty minutes.

I came hard, but not *that* fucking hard.

I glanced at her over my shoulder. She bounced happily through the workshop, still humming, and tugged on her ponytail as she went.

Her hips swayed side to side, and she skipped through the door to the staff room.

I dropped my head and sighed again. I had no idea what to do.

"Okay." She stopped, hugging her purse to her body. She'd put the sweatshirt on, covering the hem of her skirt. "I'll see you tomorrow?"

Tomorrow.

Right.

"Yeah. Sure." I smiled.

She smiled.

She walked off.

Something grabbed hold of me.

"Jamie!" I stepped over a couple things on the floor and caught her just outside the doors.

"Did I forget something?" She turned around, those bright blue eyes catching mine.

"No. I just..." Fuck me, why couldn't I get my words out. "Never mind. I forgot."

She paused, her lips twitching for a second. "Uh...Okay. See you tomorrow."

"See you tomorrow." I started back inside but stopped. "Dinner!"

Shit.

"What?"

Shit.

I turned with an awkward grimace. "Dinner. That's what I forgot. Dinner."

She dumped her purse in her car and looked at me over the top of the door. "What about dinner?"

Of course she wouldn't make this easy for me.

"I'm hungry," I said stupidly.

Jesus, apparently sex rendered me unable to string a sentence together. Was I twenty-seven or seventeen?

"Okay?" Jamie's lips pulled up at the corners, and her eyes sparkled a little too brightly.

She was doing this deliberately, and I was still too dumb to talk properly.

"Are you hungry?" Fuck, that was lame.

"Yes," she replied slowly. "Where are you going with this?"

"Nowhere fast, apparently."

She folded her arms and leaned against her car. "Dexter Ryne, are you asking me out?"

"No." I shook my head emphatically. "I'm asking if you're hungry."

"Of all the things I know about you, this awkwardness is a new one." Her eyes glittered even more. She was laughing at me silently.

Jesus, damn it.

"Do you want to get dinner with me tonight?" I spat it out before I changed my mind. Hell, I'd gone through enough awkward non-sentences to get to this point.

"Amazing." She was grinning. "You can tell me you want to fuck me without blinking an eyelid, yet asking me out for dinner takes you ten minutes to get to."

I stared at her. "I can take it back, you know."

She tilted her head to the side. "All right."

"All right?"

"I'll have dinner with you." Her smile turned a little shy. "As long as it's pizza and you bring it to my place because I'm too tired to get dressed up."

I laughed. "You got a deal."

---

"You're having dinner with her?" Roxy blinked at me. "That's the least Dex thing to ever happen."

She paused, then gasped and pointed at me. "You had sex with her!"

I threw my arms out. "Why the hell does me having dinner with her have to mean I had sex with her?"

"Well, did you?"

"That's not the point. Why are you even in my bedroom?" I grabbed a pair of jeans out of my dresser and threw them on my bed.

Why the hell was I still living with my family?

"What are you, twelve?" Roxy sat on the edge of my bed.

"Don't you have a child to look after?"

She waved her hand. "She's helping Greta make Bolognese. She's all good. I want to know about you and Jamie."

"I'm your brother. This is sick."

"You like her." She grinned, putting her elbows on her knees and propping her head up on her hands. "You like her, and that's why you don't want to talk about it."

I sighed and took off my shirt. "No, I just don't want to talk about it with *you*."

"You totally had sex with her."

"You don't know that."

"Oh, did a car put those scratches at the very top of your back?"

I froze.

Aw, shit. Jamie's nails weren't long, but they were long enough to leave a mark. And since she'd been digging them into me only a few hours ago, I knew my sister wasn't bluffing.

I grabbed a clean t-shirt and threw it over my head with a glare her way.

She grinned.

"What does it matter?" I asked, pulling off my dirty socks. I threw them in the laundry basket. "It's just food."

"Food with a girl you had sex with. In the middle of the day. You don't even call girls you sleep with, never mind take them for dinner after."

"Okay, for a start, I'm not taking her for dinner. I'm taking dinner to her." I paused. "And I don't need to take girls I've had sex with for dinner after because the food generally comes first. That's how I get them into bed."

Roxy raised an eyebrow. "Then how did you convince Jamie to have sex with you?"

"My stunning personality, clearly."

"You have a personality?"

"Get out of my room," I deadpanned. "Now."

She got up and left, laughing her ass off as she went.

I hated my sister sometimes. I couldn't believe she was fucking thirty next month.

I swung my door shut and finished getting changed. It was a miracle I'd managed a shower before Roxy had come in and started bugging me, all because I'd told Pops I didn't need dinner tonight because I had plans.

My sister had, obviously, jumped to all the right conclusions.

I finished getting ready and went downstairs.

I managed to get out unscathed and into my car where I was able to run and get pizza.

Half an hour later, I pulled up outside Jamie's house and got out of the car, pizza boxes in hand. The rich smell of melted cheese and hot bread emanated from the boxes, and my stomach rumbled before I could knock on the door.

I paused, waited for it to pass, then rapped my knuckles against the door.

Silence.

Her car was here, so she had to be home.

I knocked again.

"I'm coming!" came a shout from behind me.

I turned and saw her running down a stone path through the yard. She was wearing yoga pants, and her crazy air circled her head like a freaking mane as she came barreling toward me.

"Crap! Sorry. Shit!" She almost tripped over her own feet right in front of me, but I was quicker than her fall, and I managed to grab hold of her upper arm and steady her.

"Whoa, speedy. Where did you just come from?"

She looked up at me with slightly glazed eyes and grinned giddily. "My parents'. It's right over there." She pointed to the bigger house behind some trees.

"Are you...are you drunk?" My lips twitched.

She pouted and frowned. "Noooo. I had a little wine, but I'm not drunk. Not really drunk."

"You look a little drunk."

She pressed a finger to her lips and shushed

me. Then, as if she'd forgotten why I was here, she looked at the pizza boxes and her eyes widened. "Oh, pizza! Let's go inside. I have my keys here..." She slipped her hand inside her bra and pulled out a small brass key. "Ta-da!"

I raised an eyebrow. "You put it in your bra?"

"Yeah." She looked at me as though it was totally normal. "Where else would I put it?"

"In your pocket?" I patted mine for good measure, and my keys jingled.

"I did put it in my pocket." She touched the side of her boob. "You can keep phones, keys, cash... Literally anything in your bra."

"Can we discuss this inside? As thrilling as it is, the pizza is getting cold."

She gasped. "Shit. Okay. Yes. Hold on." She bent right forward and put the key in the door.

I mean, she tried to put the key in the door. She aimed and...missed.

"Oops." She giggled. "Hang on." She tried another two times and missed both times.

"I got it. Here, hold—never mind." I readjusted the pizza boxes and took the key from her. I got it in first try and unlocked the door. "Go on, tipsy. Inside."

"I'm not drunk!" And she tripped over the doorframe.

"No, you look perfectly sober."

She giggled behind her hands and sat on the sofa. Sighing heavily, she pulled her feet up onto the cushion and crossed her legs. Then, she peered over at me, up through her dark eyelashes, grinned, and patted the sofa next to her.

Yep.

She was drunk.

She could barely look me in the eye all afternoon.

I took the key out of the door and dropped it in the bowl next to the door before shutting it. "I'm torn between staying and making sure you don't throw up and leaving this pizza with you and trying again tomorrow."

She clapped her hands against her cheeks. "Oh my God, I'm so sorry, I ruined the date."

"It wasn't really a date. Just...dinner."

"That's a date."

"All right, fine, it was a date." I put the boxes on the coffee table and sat down next to her. "And you're drunk."

Sighing again, she rolled her eyes. "I'm not drunk. I'm just...happy."

"Happy."

"Yes, happy." She nodded her head a bit too vigorously. "See, I got home, then I realized what we did today and that we were going to have dinner together and then I panicked and raided my mom's wine stash, because can you believe there's none in my house?"

She looked at me so earnestly that I couldn't help but smile at her. Jesus, drunk Jamie was adorable...

"Shocking," I said.

She nodded in agreement. "Terrible. Anyway. I went to get a glass of wine because I was kinda nervous and next thing I know...the bottle is empty. Gone. Poof." She held out her hands. "I don't know what happened to it."

"I'm gonna say you drank it, darlin'."

She opened her mouth and then, "Yeah, yeah I did. Oops. I'm sorry."

"Don't worry." My lips twitched. "I kinda like you when you're drunk. Your cheeks go all pink and you get real cute."

"Great. Not long ago you were screwing me against a toolbox, and now you think I'm cute." She gave a suffering sigh and opened a pizza box. "Way to drop me down the totem pole."

I laughed and opened the second box. "For what it's worth, I think you're real cute anyway."

She glanced at me and giggled again.

Shit, that was the best giggle I'd ever heard, and I'd spent years babysitting Charley.

Nothing was cuter than a baby giggle. Except Jamie's tiny, drunken ones.

What the hell was I thinking? Her giggles were cute?

If Roxy had jinxed me by telling me I liked her, I was going to kill her. Slowly, painfully, and torturously.

"Okay, but really, I am sorry." She bit her lip and picked at some cheese. "I was nervous."

"Of what?" I said around a mouthful of pizza. "I'm not exactly a stranger. In fact, we're more than familiar with each other at this point."

She blushed. "I know, but we barely spoke to each other after. I knew it would be awkward. I only wanted some Dutch courage but instead I got..."

"Hammered. You got hammered."

"I got nailed earlier, so eh."

I tried not to laugh. Fuck, I tried, but I couldn't help it. She said it so flippantly that I knew for sure she was way more drunk than she was letting on.

That was not the Jamie I knew.

Then again, today had shown me a whole other side of the woman I thought I knew. And hell, she was sexy as fuck.

Adorable. Cute. Sexy.

Fuck. My sister was right.

I liked her.

I liked her a whole damn lot.

Motherfucker.

Jamie shoved some pizza in her mouth and reached over for the remote control. I only just managed to save the box from sliding onto the floor off her lap, laughing through my own mouthful of food.

When she worked, she was scarily coordinated.

When she was drunk, she was a hot mess.

I didn't know which one I liked more. The put-together, controlled woman who let the mask slip every now and then, or the one who just didn't care.

I didn't want to pick.

"Whoops." She giggled and put the box on the table. It was probably for the best. "Now," she said, pizza in one hand and remote in the other. "Do you want to watch Friends, Friends, or Friends?"

I hesitated. "God, darlin', I don't know. I can't pick between all those choices."

"Oh dear, I guess I'll pick. Friends it is!" She hit the button and squinted. "The One Where Ross Finds Out. Ooooh, yes! This is my favorite!"

I studied her for a moment. Even when she dropped the remote on the floor and nestled back with her pizza. I decided not to reveal to her my knowledge of Friends yet.

Hey. I had a sister. I'd lost too many bets and been forced to watch this as a teenager.

Shit, I'd lost one just last month, and that'd been an entire series bet.

I picked up a slice of my pizza and leaned back, watching the TV. I couldn't help the way my eyes flicked to Jamie every few minutes. Her hair was a frizzy, crazy mess, like she'd stepped right out of the shower and just left it to poof out.

I half expected her to pull out some neon leg warmers and announce she was headed to an eighties birthday party or something.

She sat in silence, nibbling her way through the pizza at a steady pace. I was going to call bullshit on her claim that she'd only had one bottle of wine.

And if it were true, she'd had something else to drink.

Still, I stayed quiet. I'd tease her about this tomorrow when she showed up to work—if she wasn't too fucking hungover to do so.

When she snorted and almost choked on her

mouthful of pizza, I had to bite back my own laugh.

Oh yeah.

I was going to tease the fuck out of her tomorrow.

# 23

## JAMIE

There was a marching band inside my head. That marching band was made up of toddlers with pans and wooden spoons, and they'd all had their favorite toy taken away, so as well, as creating a new genre of music, they were screaming like they were a new metal band.

Not to mention that my head itself weighed the equivalent of a baby elephant.

Jesus. What the hell had I done last night?

I hadn't drunk with Dex, that much I did know. Had I drunk so much at my parents' that it'd taken a while to kick in?

I rolled out of bed and walked into the front room, holding onto my head.

Wait.

Where the hell were my yoga pants? And why wasn't I wearing my bra?

Was I responsible for that, or...

God, no. Had I had sex with Dex again? Fuck, why had I thought it was a good idea to drink before he came for dinner?

The empty pizza boxes weren't in the front room, and when I stumbled blearily into the kitchen, I found them flattened on the side. A glance into the trashcan showed a couple of leftover pieces and some crust.

Good. So... I'd been sober enough to eat, right?

I scratched my forehead and started the coffee machine before wandering back into my room. There was a piece of paper on the floor, and I bent down to pick it up.

Then sat down.

Holy spinning bedroom.

I blinked, and when the dizzy sensation had passed, I opened the paper, instantly recognizing Dex's messy handwriting.

*Jamie,*
*First: Nothing happened. You threw up, so I put you to bed, where you insisted I remove your clothes and change your bra. Your panties stayed on.*

That part was underlined three times.

I appreciated the emphasis.

*Second: Thank you for the random compliment on my cock when your head was in the toilet bowl. I appreciated knowing you vomited while thinking of my dick.*

Oh, sweet fucking hell...

*Third: You owe me a date. In public. Without you being drunk.*

Wait. Who said last night was a date?
I paused as the memory flooded back.
I did.
I'd apologized for ruining our date, and he'd gone with it.
Shit...

*Four: You're probably already late when you read this, so you don't have to come to work until lunchtime...where my sister will likely accost you into lunch. And you deserve that, you little lush.*

*Dex*

Oh no, no, no...
This was why I didn't like dating. I ultimately made a fool of myself. Except this time, the guy I'd tried to have a date with was first my boss, second the guy who'd screwed me against a toolbox, and third...
Well, I wasn't even sure I liked him.
But the fact he looked after me while I vomited and put me to—
Motherfucker. He was going to be on my ass about this for as long as I lived. There was no way he'd let me live this down. What had I done, except for set myself up for almost constant ridicule?

Oh God.

This was going to be a disaster.

---

I took Dex at his word and didn't show up until lunchtime. And by taking him at his word, I mean I downed some pills, about three pints of water, and went back to bed.

After a shower and some more ibuprofen, I resembled something human. At least, I was more human than I had been when I'd woken up and read Dex's letter.

I paid the cab driver and got out. Driving was not on the agenda today. Even if it meant I had to ask Dex to drive me home.

Hell—the guy had given me an orgasm, so I'm sure a ride would be no problem.

I walked slowly toward the open garage doors and adjusted my sunglasses. At least it was bright and sunny today so they didn't look completely out of place.

Dex was leaning against the back of the Dodge, arms folded, ankles crossed, with the biggest, shit-eating grin on his face. "Good morning, Sleeping Beauty."

I groaned, shielding my face from him. "Don't."

"Don't what? Mention how you wouldn't let me leave unless I took off your yoga pants, or how you threw your bra at your light and it hung there like a Christmas decoration?"

"Stop," I moaned, walking in the direction of the coffee machine.

"Or how you spent ten minutes throwing up after Ross wrote a Con list about Rachel?"

Friends? We watched Friends?

Jesus...

"I don't want to talk about this anymore." I pressed the coffee machine button.

"Which, by the way, we never discussed this," he said, following me. "But Ross is absolutely the worst character on that show. He and Rachel never should have been together."

I gasped, clutching my chest and dropping my jaw. I spun around to face him. "How dare you swear at me!"

His eyebrows shot up. "Seriously? You can't even be his advocate. He was a selfish, obsessive, needy asshole who constantly stood in her way."

"He was her lobster!"

"Lobsters don't even mate for life." Dex rolled his eyes. "They're dirty little cheaters. Like Ross, since they weren't on a break."

I paused. "I agree with you there. And really, they don't mate for life?"

He shook his head, leaning against the doorframe. "Nope. They're monogamous, but they change partners. If Phoebe wanted to be accurate, she should have called them penguins."

I put my coffee mug under the machine and hit the button. "How...how the hell do you know so much about Friends?"

"I have a sister. I make stupid bets. I've

watched them a lot."

"Did we have this conversation last night?"

"No, darlin', we didn't. It was mostly you telling me how nervous you were to have dinner with me which lead to you getting drunk. There was a little in there about us having sex, too."

I leaned forward and slumped against the countertop, burying my face in my arms. "Oh no, no, noooo."

"I admit, my favorite part of the night was when you stopped vomiting enough to compliment my sex skills and thank me for the best orgasm of your life."

I turned my head to the side and craned to meet his eyes. "I can't decide if this is all true, or if you're just saying it to wind me up."

Dex held up his hands, then drew an invisible cross over his heart. "Cross my heart. It's all true."

"What are you crossing your heart for?" Roxy appeared behind him and looked between us.

My coffee stopped pouring, so I stood up.

Dex nodded toward me. "I'm promising her I'm not making up the drunk mess she was last night."

"Well, you do drive people to drink," Roxy replied. She pushed past him and opened the fridge. She grabbed the cream and took over making my coffee. "And, Jamie, if he's crossing his heart, he's telling the truth."

I shot Dex a skeptical side-eye. "Really?"

"Yep," Roxy answered for him. "Charley made him start doing it when she was four because he kept promising ice cream and never following through. It's habit. If he crosses his heart, he's being completely truthful."

Interesting.

"Interesting," I said. "Thank you." I took my coffee from her and sipped.

"It's not habit," Dex argued, still unmoving from his place in the doorway. "I only say when I want someone to believe me."

"Did you steal my diary and leave it in Gary Forsyth's locker in high school?" Roxy shot back.

"No."

She raised her eyebrows then turned to me. "See? Liar."

"Why are you in my garage? You're all up in my business lately. Go away."

Roxy grinned ear-to-ear. "I told you, I'm taking my friend Jamie to lunch. You just happen to be here."

Dex glared at her.

"And I'm all up in your business because you're a stubborn-ass dick," she continued, examining her nails.

He carried on glaring. "I don't think she's hungry. She just got here."

I looked between them. "No, no, I'm hungry." I couldn't be further from being hungry, but still...

I took one last swig from my mug before tipping the rest down the sink and looking at Roxy. "Let's go."

"What's good here?" Roxy browsed the menu of my favorite taco place.

"Literally everything," I replied. And now, after the drive, I was hungry.

And yes, I was eating tacos again. So shoot me. There was no such thing as too many tacos, all right?

Plus, it wasn't like I'd really had dinner last night, was it?

"All righty then." She glanced at it one more time, just as our server came up.

We both placed our orders, and I gratefully took the ice water she'd left at our table.

Roxy slid the big-ass jug of water over to the back of the booth and tore the top off the paper packaging for the straw. "So. I'm sure you're fully aware of my ulterior motive for this lunch date. Not that I don't love spending time with the person who can bring my asshole of a brother to his knees, but in the name of honesty and all that shit."

I snorted so hard I sucked water into my nose. I pinched my nostrils together and waited until the freeze had passed. "Yep. I'm pretty sure I do know, and I'm pretty sure you planned this before I got apparently blind drunk last night."

"I'd get blind drunk if I had to go on a date with him even if he wasn't my brother." She stirred the ice cubes with her straw, sipped, and edged the glass aside. Then grinned. "He told me that you two, you know, did it."

I was going to kill him.

"Um..." My cheeks flamed. "It was an accident."

"Yeah, sure. I mean, you see people tripping and shoving their dicks into random vaginas all the time."

I coughed and glanced away. "Well, it doesn't matter, because after last night..."

"Yeah, yeah, yeah. I know all about it. You got drunk because you were nervous and ended up throwing up while he held back your hair. Then he made you sip water until he was sure you were done throwing up."

"What? He didn't tell me all that."

"Of course he didn't. That makes him look too much like a decent guy." She rolled her eyes. "He stayed until you were asleep and locked your door on his way out."

"That's why my key was on the mat," I mused.

She raised her eyebrows. "Can I tell you something he'll kill me for?"

"As a rule... Please do."

Roxy laughed and sipped her water before speaking. "I think he likes you. And I don't mean as a friend."

I stilled.

What was I supposed to reply to that? Everything I knew about him pointed to the alternative. I knew he was attracted to me but was I dense to believe that he didn't like me?

Yes.

I think I was.

Because the more I learned about him, the more I liked him, too.

And I didn't quite know what to do about that.

"Oh," I said quietly. "You do?"

"You sound surprised," Roxy replied just as quietly.

"I am."

"Are you, really? Because if someone told me he liked you, I wouldn't be at all." She looked at me, but she drew circles with water droplets on the table. "He's an ass, and some of his opinions about your industry are a little backdated, but he's really not a bad person. He's just harder to break down."

I swallowed hard and looked down. I knew what she was saying was true.

He was an asshole, and his opinions were bullshit, but that didn't make him a bad person.

Horrible people didn't hold your hair while you threw up or hold you getting blind drunk in what was supposed to be a date against you.

At least, I hoped he didn't hold it against me.

My fear had definitely gotten the better of me.

The fear that the date would prove what I already knew.

That somewhere between the bickering and the bitching and the endless arguing—oh hell, during it all, too—I'd found someone I could stand up against and who could stand up against me.

And in the most unlikely place.

Again, I swallowed, and I looked away.

"You two act like you can't stand to be around each other." Roxy's voice was soft. "Yet, sometimes, I think that might be the thing you like the most."

# 24

## JAMIE

I didn't care what Roxy said. There was no way that being around Dex was my favorite thing.

That was reserved for eating tacos in my yoga pants.

"How's your hangover?"

"It wasn't a hangover," I said, setting aside the old tire. "It was a sensitivity to the sun."

Dex snorted and folded his arms. "A sensitivity to the sunlight. Is that a new thing you've developed? You haven't been sensitive the entire time we've known each other."

I cleared my throat. "We've known each other two weeks. It's a random thing."

"I bet it comes on after you've had a lot of wine, too."

"Not always." I pulled the new tire over and started fitting it. "Just...sometimes."

"So, after wine."

"Oh my God, leave me alone." I pulled my

hair so it covered my face and dipped my head so he couldn't see the little flush that raised up my cheeks.

He laughed and passed me a tool I needed. "Still hungover, then?"

"Little bit." I winced and took the tool. "Thanks."

"Tacos didn't help, then?"

"Probably would have helped a little more if my lunch date hadn't been your sister." I paused and looked up to meet his eyes. "That sounded much worse than I meant it."

Dex's lips twitched. "It always does when my sister is involved. She's not really the most stimulating conversationalist."

"No, no, the conversation was fine. Just the... topic...was off."

"What was the—never mind. I can guess."

I grimaced and nodded.

"Did she tell you all my secrets?"

"Only the one about how you used to twirl your penis like a helicopter every time you took a bath."

Dex took a deep breath, his nostrils flaring. "She's been saving that one for something special. She must really like you."

"Everyone likes me. Except you."

"I don't dislike you. In fact, I find you quite tolerable lately. As long as you're not throwing up on me."

"I thought I vomited in the toilet."

He paused. "Mostly. You kinda missed right

after you were done complimenting my cock."

I blushed. "Will you *stop* reminding me I said that?"

"Never. In fact, I think it's my new favorite thing to do." He grinned. "I'm going to bring it up every day."

I groaned and rested my forehead against the car. "I knew dinner was a bad idea."

"Wrong," he said from the staff room. The fridge opened and closed. "Dinner was an excellent idea. It was great pizza—not that you remember it. Wine was the bad idea."

"Fine, fine, whatever. Wine was the bad idea. Said no-one ever," I finished on a mutter.

"You still owe me a dinner date, by the way." He walked back out with a bottle of water in his hand. "And you agreed to it."

I finished the tire and got up to walk to him. "You really can't hold me to anything I said given that I can't remember it. And that includes the penis compliment." I took the bottle from his hand and unscrewed it.

"Says you. As far as I'm concerned, I'm believed you when you said I had a wonderful penis."

This was going from bad to worse.

"I'm slightly biased," he continued, "but I do happen to agree." Then, he patted it lightly.

"I still think you're lying."

"I crossed my heart. If you do that and you're lying, you die."

"Yeah, if you're six." I rolled my eyes. "This is ridiculous. Face it. We never should have tried to have dinner together, because we're almost incapable of having an adult conversation."

"You were pretty X-rated last night."

I glared at him. "You know what I mean. Having dinner last night, especially after what happened, was a bad idea. Admit it."

He folded his arms, and just as he opened his mouth, the phone rang.

"I got it." I darted across the garage before he could move. I answered the phone and booked in the requested M.O.T for next week before going back in.

"I don't think it was a bad idea," he said almost immediately. "Think about it. I got to see you drunk and adorable. Given that you're never that adorable sober, I saw another side of you."

"It's not my most endearing side."

"I disagree. It's the most endearing one I've seen."

I stared at him flatly. "You're beginning to piss me off."

He rubbed his mouth, but his hand couldn't hide his grin. He stepped down into the workshop and walked over to me. Stopping just inches in front of me, he hooked a finger under my chin and tilted my head back so our gazes locked.

"You still owe me dinner," he said in a low voice.

"Um." I bit the inside of my cheek. "I do?"

"Mhmm. You agreed last night, so I'm cashing in tonight."

"Right, but you also owe me for your aunt's

party, so...I think this balances out."

Dex pursed his lips. "It doesn't."

"It does."

"It doesn't."

"If you want to go on a date with me, just ask."

"I did, and you got drunk."

"You didn't specify that I couldn't. Besides, I was wearing the world's grossest panties and I needed to get rid of that memory." I paused. "You should be more specific next time you ask me out."

He raised his eyebrows. Slowly, he ran his fingertips up the curve of my jaw and pushed my hair behind my ear.

"Why do you always do that?" The words escaped me before I could think about it.

"Do what?" His fingers fell through the tips of my hair, and the strands fluttered back against my shoulder.

I lifted my hand to touch my hair. "My hair. You always tuck it behind my ear."

"Why wouldn't I?"

"Because it's so tender and that's the total opposite of everything I know about you."

He momentarily dipped his head with a smile, before lifting his gaze to meet mine again. "Because," he said softly, running his fingertips along the path they'd just taken... Along the side of my temple, curving behind my ear, down my neck. "Your hair is so crazy and... It hides your face. And I like seeing your face."

Oh.

"Oh," I squeaked. "Well, okay."

"Have dinner with me tonight. Sober dinner. Somewhere that isn't your house so it isn't awkward." He cupped my chin. "Please?"

I looked at him. Really looked at him. At his deep blue eyes that held mine so firmly, at his full lips and stubbled jaw...

"Okay." It came out a little more than a whisper. I cleared my throat and said, "But only because I owe you."

His mouth twitched. "Only 'cause you owe me."

---

I stared at the menu a little too hard. My gaze lingered on the salmon before I ultimately landed on the burger and stared a hole through the page.

This was weird. This wasn't pizza at my place, this was dinner. I was in heels. Jeans and a pretty shirt, but still heels. This made this more than dinner.

Heels made this a date.

Ugh, heels...

I was definitely a flats girl. Sneakers, flat boots, flip-flops... Give me those over back-breaking stilettos any day.

"You look like you're trying to shoot a laser through the menu with your eyes," Dex remarked.

I put the menu down. The next clue this was a date? He was wearing a shirt. No tie or jacket, but a shirt. White. Sleeves rolled to his elbows.

Top two buttons open. Fitted enough that I could perv on his biceps every time he bent his arms.

What? I was shameless. That much had already been established.

"Do you not think this is awkward?" I asked him, touching my fingers to the base of my wine glass.

All right, yes, I was a lush, but it was necessary. Hair of the dog and all that.

A few hours late, but whatever.

"You're making it awkward." His lips twisted to the side. "It's just dinner, Jamie. Friends have dinner all the time."

"We're not friends. You said so."

"True. What about non-friends who fuck? Can they have dinner?"

I leaned forward and lowered my voice. "Non-friends who fuck*ed*, you mean."

He looked at me for a moment. "No, I'm pretty sure I mean non-friends who fuck."

"Fucked," I repeated.

"You don't wanna do that again?"

I choked on my own spit. "Again?"

"No need to sound so horrified. Fucking hell."

Now, I choked on my own laughter. "I didn't mean—oh my God."

"What can I get you, folks?"

We both jolted as the server, Georgia Hopkins, appeared at our table. A grade younger than me in school, she eyed us both as we shared a look and I picked back up my menu.

"I'll have the ten-ounce rump steak." Dex shut

his menu and handed it back to her.

"And for you?" she asked, flicking her red hair over her shoulder.

"The cheeseburger. Thanks." I gave her the menu without looking at her.

What? She'd stolen my boyfriend once upon a time.

I'd been sixteen, but a boyfriend stealer was a boyfriend stealer, my friend.

Dex raised an eyebrow at me.

"She stole my boyfriend in sophomore year."

"Ouch."

"Kinda. He got busted for drugs three years later and she was in his car." I sipped my wine. "That was fun."

"Small towns," he muttered. "Bunch of weirdos."

"Hey!" I threw my napkin across the table at him. "I'm not weird. I'm simply...unforgiving. I remember shit."

"That doesn't bode well for me, does it?"

"What? After you fire me next week?" I leaned back. "I don't care. You were always going to fire me."

His hand hovered around the base of his beer glass. "Was I?"

"Based on everything I know about you? Yes."

"What if you don't know me at all?"

I watched him for a moment.

How his fingers twitched against the table.

How his eyelashes fanned over his cheeks when he blinked.

How his teeth grazed over his lower lip.

"Then I don't know," I admitted, twirling the stem of my glass. "You're just fucking with me now."

"How am I fucking with you? We don't really know anything about each other. We bickered too much."

"Are you saying we should get to know each other?"

"You sound horrified about all my suggestions."

"Well, they are a little out of character."

His lips twitched. "I told you. You don't really know me that well. You know know—"

I pointed toward the door. "If you bring up what I said while intoxicated, I swear to God, I will walk right out of that door."

His laughter filled the air and he shook his head. "All right, all right. I won't bring it up. Right now."

"You've brought it up enough times today. Any more than two and it's ridiculous."

"I am ridiculous. You know that."

I tilted my glass toward him. "Now, that I can agree on." I sipped, meeting his eyes. "You really want to get to know each other?"

"You already asked me that." A smile stretched his lips.

"I know. Just double checking."

He flattened his hands on the table, palms up and fingers splayed. "We work together. You... might be proving me wrong... So, why not?"

Folding my arms, I sat back in my chair and

eyed him. I didn't believe him—I felt like there as an ulterior motive that I couldn't figure out, but I'd play along.

Our entire relationship was based on us playing along with each other, after all. If it wasn't broken, why fix it?

"Fine," I said slowly. "Let's do that...for whatever reason, you aren't telling me."

Laughter danced in his eyes. "What's your favorite movie?"

"Really? We're going to do twenty questions?"

Dex paused. "I could probably think up twenty questions if you wanted me to."

"I didn't say I wanted you to."

"I think I have twenty now."

Dear God, no.

"What's your favorite movie?" he repeated.

I sighed. Was I really going to do this? Yes. Yes, I was. "That's tough. I don't really watch movies."

"You don't watch movies?"

I shook my head. "I prefer TV shows. But if I really had to pick...I don't know. Home Alone?"

"Are you asking me if that's your favorite?" A tiny smirk formed on his face.

"I'm just throwing it out. I do watch it about fifty times every Christmas, so I guess it's my favorite." I paused. "What's yours?"

"Power Rangers. The original. No contest."

"Really?"

"Yeah. I always wanted to be the black one. Everyone I knew wanted to be red." He smiled as he took a sip of his beer. "Favorite food?"

"Tacos. I thought that was obvious."

"Mine, too. See—we have something in common."

"We're both mechanics who like tacos. Hold the press—that's front-page news." I rolled my eyes.

"It's a start." He grinned. "Favorite color?"

Oh Jesus, he was serious about the twenty questions thing.

"Don't have one. Yours?"

"Whatever color lipstick you're wearing."

I stared at him. "That was either really cheesy, or a lame attempt at a pick-up line. Or both."

He shrugged a shoulder. "I admit, it wasn't my best. What's your favorite pizza topping?"

I blinked. "You're just asking me things you already know now. Are you really going to make me sit through twenty questions?"

He grinned, and I knew the answer.

Yes.

Yes, he was.

---

Two hours later, we were lying on the grass in the park, and I knew far more about Dexter Ryne than I knew about myself.

I knew he hated anything tomato until he was fifteen. He couldn't swim until he was eight, and he still, to this day, wouldn't swim underwater because he almost drowned when he was six. I knew he preferred the rain over the sun, but he hated being cold, and I knew that he hated long toenails with a passion.

Just like he knew I loved brussel sprouts but couldn't stand carrots. He knew I hated being hot and owned twenty-seven pairs of thick and fluffy socks. He also knew that I was a ballet dancer when I was younger but now could barely hold a tune to the Macarena, and nothing freaked me out more than spider webs.

Dinner had been this weird mish-mash of facts, and it'd only continued as we'd left the restaurant and walked to the park, even as we'd detoured to grab coffee.

Dex knocked over his empty cup as he rolled onto his side and propped his head up on his hand. "I need to know. How do you store your sugar and salt if you baked a cake with salt?"

"Ugh, okay." I dropped my head down to the grass before jerking it back up. "So, my mom is a total neat-freak. She has this serious organizational system in the pantry, and basically, everything that gets bought has its own jar, and they all have these little chalk signs attached to the front of them."

"I think I can see where this is going."

"I pulled out both the jars and even tasted it, then got distracted by my mom's cat being up on the counter. Long story short, I forgot which one was which, and accidentally put the sugar away."

"You didn't think to check again?"

"Hey—I was sixteen and was trying to stop

a cat sitting in my bowl of flour. I had some priorities. Like not baking cat hair."

He waved his hand. "So, you didn't know until you ate it?"

I grimaced. "Nope. The worst part is that this was when my parents weren't together. I never got along with my stepmom, and it was her birthday cake."

Dex shook as he held back laughter.

"I'd been a bit horrible to her when I'd stayed at my dad's, so the birthday cake was my way of trying to build a bridge and..."

"You burned it down."

I nodded. "She thought I'd done it deliberately and wouldn't listen to reason that it was a mistake."

"Oh man. That's horrible."

"Not really. My mom knew I was a terrible baker, and later admitted to coming into the kitchen while I was chasing the cat out and switching the jars." I smirked. "Technically, I didn't get it wrong. She made a habit of trolling my stepmother, and that was the day she'd won."

He let the laughter go. "That's fucking amazing. Holy shit. How didn't you know?"

"I have a love-hate relationship with the cat. Sometimes she won't leave me alone, other times, she won't go near me and will hiss at the sound of my voice."

"That sounds like my sister."

I nudged him in the shoulder and rolled over onto my back. "She's not that bad."

"Nah, she's not. But she did hiss at me once. I slipped a naked baby photo of her in her boyfriend's pocket. It didn't matter, but he was the asshole who knocked her up."

"Am I nosy if I say I wondered about that?"

He shook his head. "She's the first person to tell the story. She's not ashamed of the fact she's a single parent. She said she'd rather it than have to fight with a total jackass all the time. She did that for a year before she realized she was giving him energy that she could have spent on Charley."

"He never sees her?"

"He's met her about three times. It doesn't really matter. Charley doesn't need him, and neither does Roxy."

Despite the arguing, he softened when he spoke about them. It was plain to see they were as close as siblings could be.

"She's got you." I smiled, turning my face toward him.

He shrugged, brushing it off. "I'm not that great."

"Oh, sure. Everything else, you brag about, but being a great uncle and brother? No, you're a terrible person."

He laughed, pushing hair from my face. "It's so nice when we agree."

I batted his hand away. "I'm not agreeing with you. That was called sarcasm, you nut."

"I know. It's been a while since I fucked with you, that's all."

I glared at him. "Stop, or I'll call your sister

and make her tell me more about how you used to play with your penis in the bathtub."

"No." He covered his eyes with his forearm. "Don't do that. She'll take out a column in the local newspaper if she thinks enough people care about it."

"Hm. That's tempting." I set up and reached for my purse.

"Don't you dare."

I leaned right over and grabbed it.

Dex jumped on top of me. I squealed and gripped hold of the straps, but he was stronger than me, and he easily wrestled the straps from my grip and tossed it to the side.

"Nooo!" I laughed, stretching my arm out, but he was straddling me now, and he grasped my wrists and pinned them to the ground above my head. I wriggled against his hold, eventually giving up to pout at him.

He grinned like the cat who had the cream. "Yes. You're not calling her."

I pouted harder. "I was messing. And now you're squashing me. Can I have my hands back?"

His eyes searched mine. "I don't know. I'm still deciding."

"Deciding? What is there to decide? If I can have back the use of my own hands?"

"No. Deciding if I should kiss you or not."

My heart skipped a beat. "Do I have a say in that?"

"Do you care either way?"

"I—I mean, maybe. I don't—"

"That's a no, then."

I nodded.

He stared at me a little longer, his fingers twitching as they held my wrists together. The grass tickled against my skin, but all I could really focus on was the way his eyes pierced mine—on the battle that waged in his eyes.

I wanted to reach up and grab him, to pull his mouth to mine. But I couldn't.

Thankfully, I didn't need to try.

Dex moved, lowering his mouth to mine. I leaned my face up until our lips met, and as his descended down onto mine, my head sank back into the grass. I drew a deep breath when he pulled back briefly, and our eyes met for a flash before he kissed me again.

It was warm and soft, the gentlest kiss he'd ever given me, and heat twirled slowly through my body. It was dark and there was a light chill in the fall air, but I could barely tell. Whether it was just the heat of his body over mine or the kiss or both, I didn't know, but it felt good.

So damn good.

Until I remembered something.

We were in the middle of the park.

In the middle of town.

In public.

I jerked my face away from Dex's, gasping. "Oh my God, get off me."

"What? What did I do?" He released my hands and moved.

My cheeks burned red-hot, and I sat up,

clapping my hands to my face. "Oh my God, you just kissed me in public."

"No," he deadpanned. "I thought it was in your bedroom."

"Oh my God, if anyone saw me, they'll be texting my mother right this second."

"And there goes my erection." Dex sighed and, bending one knee, hugged his leg to his chest. "Thanks for that."

"Oh God, oh God, oh God." I rocked a little. "Do you not understand how much she's going to be on my back about this? She's going to bug me all the time."

He stared at me. "You're a grown woman. You can kiss a man in public if you want."

"That was half-porn!"

"You think that was half-porn? Darlin', if you want me to show you what that is, I'd be more than happy to climb back on top of you and demonstrate."

"No. No." I stood and grabbed the empty coffee cups, then threw them in the trashcan just a few feet from us. My purse was next. "Oh God."

I looked around the park. There were tons of people. Nobody was looking at us, of course. And we were in a darker area, after all. But still.

Shit. All it took was one person. One nosy asshole walking their dog and...boom. I was in trouble with my mother.

Dexter Ryne would surely be the death of me.

# 25

## DEX

She looked like a deer in headlights. Like she'd been caught fucking me in broad daylight, not kissing me in the darkness.

I recognized it for what it was.

She didn't care if her mom knew.

She cared that, yet again, she'd liked it. That this date she wouldn't refer to as a date, one she stressed she did under duress, was more than what she would admit to.

That she liked it when I kissed her.

I knew. I'd felt it. I'd tasted it.

And I wasn't done with her. Not tonight.

"All right. We're done here." I stood up. "I'll take you home."

She drew in a deep breath, turning around to look at me. "Oh."

"Let's go." I approached her, and before she could move, grabbed her. I wrapped one arm around her back and bent to hook my other arm beneath her knees.

I picked her up.

She screamed.

"Dex! What the—what the hell are you doing?" She wrapped one arm around my neck and gripped my shirt with her other hand. She clung to me like I'd drop her any second.

"Shit! I'm dropping you!" I moved as if I was going to let her go.

She screamed again, louder, and almost strangled me with the tightness of her grip.

"I'm taking you home, and finishing what I almost started before your freak-out." I stalked toward where we were parked.

"You are not carrying me all the way to your car!"

"Oh, darlin', I am."

"You are not!"

"Yet here you are, in my arms, being carried." I grinned and caught the eye of a familiar, older man, clutching a leash with a Jack Russell on the other end. "Mr. Daniels." I nodded to him.

He nodded back silently, staring as I carried Jamie right past him.

"Oh God," she moaned, resting her head on her arm and turning her face into my shoulder. "This is so humiliating."

"You wouldn't come if I didn't make you."

"Is that a double entendre?"

"It'll be reality in about thirty minutes when I get my hands on you...somewhere you won't be worried about your mother finding out."

"Oh God. If I don't go home..."

"Darlin', you're going home. And I'm not leaving until you're too tired to make me."

"Oh God."

---

When I drove past her parents' house, no cars were outside. Jamie visibly relaxed, and I smirked as I turned off their driveway onto her extended one. I didn't understand this set-up, but boy, was I glad I didn't have to worry about parents.

Or making her be quiet.

When we'd fucked in the garage, it'd been raw. Rushed and desperate. Pure, hard passion that overtook everything else.

Tonight, it'd be different.

I knew her as a person now. I knew what she liked and what she hated. I knew fears and quirks, crazy stories from her childhood, just as she knew mine.

Now, I wanted to know more.

Wanted to know what she looked like without clothes on. Wanted to know if she was a sheet-grabber, or if she was a born scratcher. I wanted to explore her body properly, to know her outer shell as intimately as I was starting to know her inner one.

I pulled up next to her Mustang and put the truck in park. We both got out, and I walked her to the front door. "Do you need help to unlock your door this time?"

"I've got it, thank you," she said sharply, but her lips twitched into a smile as she put the key in the door and twisted it. She bit the inside of her cheek as she looked over at me. "I guess you're coming in?"

"Do you want me to go?" I met her eyes.

She looked at me for the longest moment, hand clutching the door handle. Her tongue flicked out over her lower lip, and the battle shone in her eyes.

She did, but she didn't.

She wanted me, but she was scared.

I opened my mouth to tell her I'd go, to do the opposite of the very thing I wanted. The opposite of the need that was burning through my veins right in that moment.

But she beat me to it.

She took a step closer to me, cupped the back of my neck, and lifted her lips to meet mine. The kiss was hard and full-on, one touch that I felt down to my fucking bones as she answered my question without words.

She pulled back and shoved open the door. "Okay!" Her voice was a little too high-pitched. "Come in."

I choked back a laugh, locked my car, and then closed the door behind me.

She discarded her shoes, keys, and purse on the floor and coffee table. "Do you want a drink? Something to eat? Should we turn on the—"

I grabbed her hand and pulled her against me. "I want you."

"Oh. Okay. I just—"

My fingers dove into her hair as I kissed her. She'd talk for hours if I'd let her, but I wasn't going to. I only had hours for one thing, and that thing was exploring her body. That thing was making her come, over and over, enjoying every inch of her until she begged me for sleep.

She gasped and pulled back. "Upstairs to the left."

I scooped her up again, this time over my shoulder. She squealed once more as I clamped my arm around her thighs and moved toward the stairs.

"Will you stop manhandling me?"

"Maybe, but we move quicker when I make you move, and I don't have a lot of time to waste."

"Why?" she asked, pulling my t-shirt up my back. "Are you on curfew?"

"Ha ha. No. But we both have to be up early for work, and given your late appearance today, you owe me hours. Hours I'll be happy to forget about if you shut your smart mouth and do as I say."

"Do as you say? Are you into that kinky 'sir' shit? Oh hell, do I have to call you 'sir?' You can shove that up your—"

I pushed open the first door on your left. "Jamie, this is your towel closet."

"Um. I meant on the right."

"And you say I'm bad with directions," I muttered, swinging the door shut and walking the few paces to her bedroom door.

Her supposed bedroom door.

Thankfully, it was, and I carried her through the door into the room. I paid no attention to it except for the huge bed in the middle of the room.

"You are terrible at directions. You never listen," she said, pushing the door shut over my shoulder.

I dropped her unceremoniously onto her bed. She landed with an "oomph," bounced and looked up at me. "Then it's your lucky day. The one thing I won't need directions for is your clit."

"That's a bold promise." She propped herself up and looked me up and down. "All right. If we're doing this again, get naked."

"If? There's no if about it."

"You're still wearing clothes."

I unbuttoned my shirt slowly. "So are you."

"I didn't tell myself to get naked. I told you."

"You're awfully bossy. Do you know that?"

She blinked those wide, blue eyes at me. "Actually, yes, I do. In about ten minutes, I'll be putty in your hands, so I'm all about telling you what to do while I still have my wits about me."

"That's the hottest thing you've ever said to me."

"Shut up and finish taking your clothes off."

"Take off your pants," I shot back.

She lifted her ass and shoved the jeans down her legs. That left her in that black leather jacket I loved and her lace shirt. It was a strangely sexy look—probably because there was something about the combination of her red lips, her white shirt, the black jacket, and her black underwear.

Deliberate? Maybe.

I was going to rip her out of all of it anyway.

I tossed my shirt to the side, then finished getting undressed until I was in nothing but my boxers. "Now the jacket," I told her.

She grazed her teeth over her lower lip as she shrugged it off and threw it to the side. That left her sitting in nothing but her shirt and her black thong, but that was still one item too many.

I stared pointedly at her shirt until she got the hint and pulled it off with a grin.

I approached her, but she was quicker. She literally yanked me down over her and kissed me, curling her arms around my neck as her teeth grazed my lower lip. Her body melded against mine as she deepened the kiss.

For someone so reluctant to have dinner with me...

I pushed the thought from my mind and kissed her back. My fingers wound in her hot mess hair, and I ran my other hand up the side of her nearly-naked body. She was perfection, all curves and temptation, and my fingers probed her skin as I explored her.

She wrapped her legs around my waist, pulling my cock to press against her pussy. I wanted to slide those panties aside and push inside her. Just the thought of being inside her again made my cock rock-hard, and it pushed against my boxers—and her.

She wriggled beneath me. I nipped at her

lower lip before I dragged my mouth from hers. I kissed along her jaw, down the curve of her neck, over the dip of her collarbone to her chest. Her white bra pushed her tits together, and I reached between them to unclasp it.

She gasped as I circled her nipple with my tongue. I grinned as she arched her back, pushing it harder against the tip of my tongue.

She was right.

She was already putty in my hands.

I wasted no time moving down her body and taking hold of her underwear. I slid the thong down her legs and she kicked it off to the side.

I met her eyes and grinned, parting her legs. She blushed, but lifted her head to mine so I could kiss her again. I kissed her until my cock throbbed and once again, slid down her body to the apex of her thighs.

"Oh God," she whispered, throwing her forearm over her eyes.

I kissed the top of her thigh. "I've barely touched you and you're already saying my name."

She laughed, but I cut it short when I ran my tongue along her wet pussy. Instead she gasped, and I grinned, grasping her thighs to hold her legs apart. She wriggled, but she didn't move away as I took her pussy in my mouth and explored her with my tongue.

The tiny moans that left her mouth as I focused on her clit made my heart thump. I wanted her so fucking bad, I could barely focus. I wanted this pussy around my cock. I wanted her moans in my mouth or my ear, not into the thin air. I wanted these legs around my waist while I fucked her blind, not pinned to the bed while I licked her.

Her moans grew louder. Higher. The sheet tightened under me, and when I glanced up, her knuckles were white as she grabbed hold of it.

I slid my hands under her ass and pushed her clit into my mouth. I sucked, circled, licked, teased until her entire body went tense and she cried out. It was something fucking else, hearing her moan like that. Being totally focused on nothing but her pleasure. Nothing else mattering other than the way she tensed and tightened and moved against my tongue as she rode it out.

I wiped my mouth with my hand and kissed her. She groaned, but she fisted her fingers in my hair. Pure desire thundered through my veins as she flicked her tongue against my lips. I knew she was tasting herself, and for some reason, her insistence to kiss me deeper and harder turned me the fuck on.

"I need a condom," I murmured against her mouth.

"Top drawer," she murmured back.

I moved left.

"Other top drawer." She giggled.

"Excellent directions, yet again." I opened the top drawer to the sound of her husky laughter and found the box. It was full, and I paused for only a second before I smirked and opened it.

I snatched one out and went through the motions of putting it on before I situated myself back between her legs. She bit her lip and let it go, then grabbed me again, pulling me to her and wrapping her legs around my waist.

I reached between us and pushed my cock into her.

I stopped, and she shoved off the bed.

We flipped.

My ankle hit the banister at the end of her bed, but I didn't have a chance to say anything, because Jamie was now on top of me, legs either side of my hips, with my cock buried completely inside her.

Her hands made indents into the mattress either side of my head. She grinned down at me, her crazy hair falling in a curtain around us.

I just stared at her—her shining eyes, her flushed cheeks, her parted, smiling lips—then slid my hand up her back and kissed her. My hand formed a fist in her hair, and she moved her hips up and down, her pussy tightening each time she took me again.

Kisses. Hands. Grabbing. Nails. Scratching. Heat.

It was fucking insane how she moved, taking me deeper and quicker as time moved. My hands slid from her hair to her hips, and as desperation pumped through me and my balls tightened, I grabbed her full hips, stilled her, and took control.

I pounded my cock into her, holding her in the same position. She gasped and moaned almost at the same time. Her arms gave out and her forehead dropped to my shoulder. Her pussy was so wet and tight that I groaned every time I held her in place over me.

"Oh my God, oh my God," she moaned. She grabbed my arms and her nails dug right in, and she tensed completely, crying out.

I held her hips against mine and thrust into her until I came, too. I snaked my arms around her spent body, still on top of mine, and pressed a lazy kiss to the side of her head.

We stayed like that for a moment, just holding each other. I didn't want to move unless I absolutely had to, but Jamie pulled herself up and off me, only to slump on the bed next to me.

She was breathing heavily, and when I turned my head to look at her, she turned hers and met my eyes. "Hi."

I laughed, peeling the condom off. "Hi."

"I need to pee." She rolled over and stood up too quickly. Her knees buckled, and she immediately dropped back onto the bed, making me laugh again. She flipped me the bird and tried again a few seconds later, this time taking it slower.

She managed to make it out of the bedroom.

Still laughing, I stood up myself and searched for a trashcan. I found one by the door, so I dropped the condom in it and retrieved my boxers from the floor.

I grabbed my jeans and paused. Should I put them on now? Should I wait for her to come back?

Fuck. This was why mixing work and pleasure wasn't good. I didn't want her to think I was fucking her and running. Not only would it be awkward tomorrow, it wasn't true. I just didn't damn well know what to do.

"I didn't lock the door when we came in. I just did—" Jamie stopped in the doorway, a light-blue robe wrapped around her body. It barely skimmed her thighs, and she clutched it closed at her chest. Not only had she locked the door, she'd braided her hair on the way back. "Oh. Uh, are you leaving?"

"I don't know?" I cleared my throat when I realized how dumb that answer sounded. "I don't know. Would you prefer if I did?"

"I don't, um. I don't know." She clutched the robe tighter and leaned against the doorframe. "Do you think you should?"

"It's your house, darlin'. Your house, your choice."

I wanted to stay. But I wanted her to want me to. I wanted to know what she actually wanted when it came down to it.

Her cheeks flushed, and she looked down, holding tight to the robe. She twirled her big toe across the wooden floor in circles, chewing on her lower lip.

"Does it feel weird to you?" she asked, not looking up.

"Weird?"

"Dex, three days ago, we fought over coffee. Now you might stay over?"

I held up my jeans. "It's weird, I know. I'll leave, okay?"

"No. I mean—" she stopped, then sighed.

"Jesus fucking Christ."

I laughed quietly, because that about summed it up.

Jamie pushed off the doorframe and walked over to me. She stopped just a foot or two in front of me and fiddled with the belt of the robe. "I don't—do you want to stay?"

I pushed her bangs from her eyes and ran my fingers down the side of her face. "I don't want to leave," I said quietly.

She glanced away, then looked up at me with her blue eyes shining. "Then, stay."

I dipped my head and kissed her. My stomach tightened when she moved closer, her soft fingertips brushing over my hips. She sighed when I pulled back, and I smiled down at her, loving the way her eyes lit up when our gazes met.

Jesus, what was happening?

"Okay, um." She bit her thumb, stepping back. "I'm going to get some water. Do you want some? Or coffee? Or..."

"Water is great." I fought my smile, but she was so fucking adorable when she was awkward. The side I was seeing of her right now was a million mils away from the Jamie I'd come to know.

I loved them both.

Jesus—shit—did I just say that?

No.

I didn't.

There was no way. It was a figure of speech. A manner of words. That was all.

Fucking...

"Here." She passed me a glass of water. "Oh, hey, could you turn on that lamp so I can turn this off?"

I looked at the light switch. "Sure." I put the glass on the nightstand and pressed the button on the lamp to switch it on.

"Thanks." She flashed me a smile and walked over to the other side of the bed. "Do you, um, do you have a side?"

"Do you have a side?" I fired back.

"Somewhere in the middle, usually. Sometimes diagonally. It depends."

I looked at the floor. "Do you have a blanket for when I need to set up camp on your floor?"

She laughed, setting down her glass and moving the sheets aside. "No, you're fine. I'm not as bad when I'm not alone."

"How often are you not alone?"

"Oooh. Did that hit a nerve?"

I frowned at her. "No. Just a question."

"It sounds like I hit a nerve."

"Jamie."

"What?"

I leaned over the bed and, with one arm, scooped her down onto her back. She shrieked and held her own arm out. Water splashed over us, and I laughed, taking the glass from her.

"What?" she said, looking up at me.

"Shut up." I kissed the tip of her nose and rolled over to the other side. I got under the covers as Jamie shed her robe and climbed into bed in nothing but panties and a strappy t-shirt.

"You should know," she said, turning her head to face me. "I hate being touched when I sleep, so don't touch me when I sleep."

My lips twitched. "You got it."

"At all." She opened her eyes wider as if to emphasize it.

"You got it, darlin'. I just said that." I took a mouthful of my water and turned off the lamp.

Darkness swathed the room. The only sound was us both breathing in and out, followed by the creaks of the bed springs as Jamie rolled onto her side.

A minute passed before she scooted toward the middle of the bed.

I glanced over at her although I couldn't see anything.

She moved closer to me.

"Any reason you're creeping at me?" I asked.

"Um...I'm not asleep?" she replied.

"And your point is?"

"I'm not asleep. And I'm cold. And you're not."

I fought back the laugh. "You don't like being hot."

"I don't like being cold much, either."

This time, I let the laugh go. I rolled over and moved into the middle of the bed until her back was tucked against my chest and she'd slipped one of her feet between my legs. The other was outside the covers, and I rested my arm over the covers, holding her softly against me.

I buried my face in the back of her neck,

breathing in the lingering smell of sex on her skin and the vanilla scent that clung to her hair.

I didn't want to let her go, and that terrified me.

Jamie tensed, and I knew she was about to say something. "Dex?" she whispered.

"Mm?"

"What are we doing?"

"I'm trying to sleep. I don't know about you."

She tapped my hand. "Not...literally. I mean... what are *we* doing? This."

I held her tighter. "I don't know. Do you?"

"No." She sighed. "That's what I was afraid of."

"It doesn't matter right now." Because I needed to figure out what the hell I was feeling before I knew what I was doing. "Go to sleep, beautiful."

She nestled in closer to me, pushing her ass right to my cock, and judging by the resounding silence, she did just that.

# 26

## DEX

I'd barely been able to get out of the bathroom before Jamie had shoved me out of the way to get a shower. Of course, my boxers were in the bathroom, and when I'd tried to retrieve them, she'd told me where to stick it.

Because seeing her in the shower was over the line.

*Women.*

I tightened the towel around my waist and searched through her kitchen cupboards for two mugs. I'd seen her without coffee way too many times. That meant I was smart enough to know I needed to make her one for when she was done in the shower.

I finally found them in the cupboard next to the fridge and grabbed two. They were both pink with flowers on, and a quick search turned up nothing else.

Good to know she kept the profanity-laden ones for work.

I took a minute to figure out her machine, then started to make hers. When it was done, I set her mug to the side, started my own coffee, then added her cream and sugar.

I twisted, loosening my towel. I grabbed hold of it and tightened it once again. Jesus, I really needed my boxers. This dark-purple towel was doing absolutely nothing for me, and there wasn't a chance in hell the floral, pink mug would make it better.

I sighed and put the cream back in the fridge. My coffee took the last of the sugar in the jar, and just to be a dick, I turned the jar so the "sugar" label was completely obvious.

The last thing I wanted to do was be here in the future and have salt in my coffee.

Shit. Was I thinking about the future?

With her?

I was.

Fuck. That was—

The kitchen door squeaked open, and I grabbed Jamie's coffee. "Hey, I—"

Except it wasn't Jamie.

She looked like Jamie. She had the same blue eyes and the same wild hair, but she was older.

Holy shit.

It was her mother.

And I was wearing nothing but a purple towel...and holding a pink fucking flowery mug.

"Oh." She pressed her hand to her mouth, then to her chest. "I'm so sorry. I didn't expect to—well."

I'd never been so embarrassed. What the fuck did I do now? Put down the mug and introduce myself? Did I shake her hand while virtually naked?

I felt like I'd stepped into one of those stupid chick movies I'd been forced to watch by Roxy.

We stared at each other for a moment.

"You must be Jamie's mom," I said, awkwardly gripping my towel. The last thing I needed was for it to come untucked...

"Yes." She blinked, long eyelashes framing her eyes. "I'm very sorry to say I don't recognize you."

I hesitated before I put Jamie's mug back down. "Dexter Ryne. It's lovely to meet you, Mrs. Bell." I held my hand out then pulled it back quickly. "Never mind."

Her glossy lips twisted into an amused smile. "Dexter Ryne. Now, that's a name I've heard recently."

Oh, this was going from fucking bad to fucking worse.

"I'd like to assume they're all good, but if you heard it from your daughter, I doubt it."

"Yet here you are, basically naked in her kitchen."

I shifted side-to-side. "Yes, well, I don't mean to be rude, but I'd like to put some pants on before we continue this conversation."

"Don't get dressed on my account, dear. I've seen much worse wandering around wearing much less."

Oh Jesus.

I backed toward the door, picking up Jamie's mug again. "I'll just go let her know you're here." I let go of my towel to point upstairs like an idiot, meaning the towel slipped a tiny bit. I grabbed it, turned...

And I ran like the fucking wind. I took the damn stairs two at a time, somehow managing to not spill her coffee, and shoved my way into the bathroom.

"What are you—"

"Your mother is in your kitchen!" I hissed at her in the shower. "Your mother."

"What?" she shrieked. She wiped her hand on the glass door to clear the condensation. "What the fuck are you talking about?"

"Your mother is in your kitchen. More specifically, your mother just walked in on me in your kitchen."

Jamie glanced up and down at my body, shrieked again, and covered her mouth with both hands. She stayed frozen for a moment before she shut off the shower and stepped out. "No. She's in my kitchen?"

"You want me to say it again?"

She grabbed a clean towel from the top of the toilet and wrapped it around her body. "No, no, I understand what you're—oh God, she walked in on you? Like that?"

I shoved the mug at her then snatched my boxers from the floor. "No, I was stark naked."

"You weren't."

"No, I had the towel. But I did excuse myself

to put on some pants before we continued our introduction, and she told me she'd seen "a lot worse wearing a lot less" and now I think I need therapy."

Jamie slumped back against the counter that held her sink. "No, no, no. This is not happening. This is so embarrassing."

"You're embarrassed? Your mother just saw me half-naked!"

She looked up at me. "There are worse things to see than you naked."

"Jamie, I'm never going to be able to look your mother in the eye."

"Neither am I. She's here because she knows we kissed last night and your truck is—Jesus, your truck! She did it deliberately!" Her jaw dropped. "It's parked right out front. She knew I wasn't alone. Of all the—"

"You said you locked the door!"

She put down the mug and clapped her hands against her cheek. "I did lock the door. She has a spare key. Oh, the violation."

"Can we remember that I'm the one she walked in on?"

Jamie blinked at me for a moment. "But I'm the one who'll get the grilling. Starting with, "So, darling, why was your boss and the man you insist you hate standing naked in your kitchen this morning?""

"Well, to be fair, that is a very good question."

"You're giving me whiplash!" She pointed at me and stalked into her room.

I followed her in there and shut the door. "Do I need to barricade that door with a chair, or are we safe up here?"

"I don't even know." She yanked some items out of the top drawer of her dresser. "Dex, help. I don't know what to do."

"Neither do I. Can I hide up here while you deal with it?"

"Oh, sure." She quickly dried herself with the towel before tossing it aside and grabbing her panties off the bed. "You, the big alpha male, sit up here, and I'll go and deal with the big scary mommy."

"You're no wimp. You're pretty alpha yourself. And it's your mom."

She yanked her bra straps up her arm and clasped it. A quick, rough adjustment of her boobs and she pointed a finger at me. "You're the one who made me go out with you last night. You're the one who brought me upstairs and stayed over. You are the one who is taking the fall for this with me."

"I already took it. That was the most awkward moment of my life, and I was once a teenage boy." I pulled my jeans up my legs and buttoned them. "This is unfair."

"Your penis partially got us into this," Jamie continued, buttoning her shorts.

"And we're all very lucky it didn't make an appearance this morning."

She tugged her shirt over her head. "So, you have to deal with getting us both of it. Tough

277

shit. If you ever want to consider walking around my house in a towel again, you will get your butt downstairs."

"Trust me," I said, putting my white shirt back on and buttoning it. "I will never walk around your house in a towel again. Sex or no sex."

She paused. "That's probably for the best."

---

Twenty minutes later, we both made our way downstairs. Since Jamie had jumped out of the shower without washing the conditioner out of her hair in her panic, she had to stick her head back under the water to get it out, then finish getting ready for work. I planned to stick there just long enough to get through the embarrassment, then go home to change before opening the garage.

I hovered a few feet behind Jamie. We walked into the kitchen to find her mom sitting at the table, flicking through a glossy magazine, and sipping coffee.

"Mom," Jamie started. "What are you doing here?"

"I can't stop in on my daughter before she goes to work?"

Jamie blinked at her. "Sure, you can, but this is the first time you've ever done it."

Her mom glanced at me. "Don't be silly, darling. I don't do it often, but I do it."

"No, you don't. Now, tell me what you're doing."

"Fine." She sighed. "Your father wanted to know who the truck belonged to. I have to say, I'm surprised."

"Join the club," I muttered, reaching for what was once my coffee. It already looked like it was congealing, so I tipped it straight into the sink, then turned to Jamie. "Look—I have to run home and change, all right?"

She glared daggers at me.

I hesitated before I kissed the side of her head. "I'll see you in an hour?"

She continued to glare at me.

"Mrs. Bell, it was a pleasure." I gave her an awkward wave and made sure I grabbed my keys out of my pocket before I'd even left the house.

That didn't stop me hearing Jamie's mom demand to know everything.

I ran into my truck and tore away from her house like if I didn't, Jamie would follow me outside and drag me back in to finish that conversation.

That was not happening this morning.

I drove across town to my house. I'd barely pulled up behind my sister's car when the front door opened, and Aunt Greta stood there, her surprisingly tiny frame seeming to fill the entire space.

"Where have you been?" she said before I'd even shut the car door.

"I stayed with a friend last night."

Her eyes narrowed. "You don't have any friends."

Thanks, Greta.

"I have a couple. Can I come and get changed? I have to go to work."

Greta stretched her arms out and grabbed the doorframe. "Not until you tell me where you were last night."

"Oh, Christ." Roxy stopped behind her. "Aunt Greta, he had dinner with Jamie last night. Where do you think he stayed?"

Her eyes widened. "You took her to dinner and then slept with some hussy?"

I dropped my chin to my chest and shut my eyes.

"No, Aunt Greta," Roxy said. "He slept with Jamie."

"Thanks," I snapped.

"Oh." Aunt Greta tilted her head to the side. "As long as you used protection."

"Yes," I ground out. "We used protection."

She paused. "All right. You come and get ready to work, dear."

I slipped past her and headed straight for the stairs. First, Jamie's Mom. Now, Aunt Greta. Was this indicative of how this day was going to go? Because I wasn't a fan of it.

For the second time this morning, I took a set of stairs two at a time. Then I slammed the door to my bedroom so everyone would know to leave me alone.

Not that it stopped my sister barging in like it was her room.

I threw my shirt into my laundry basket.

"What?"

"You really stayed at Jamie's?"

"Nah, Rox, I slept in my truck on her drive." I grabbed a clean t-shirt from the drawer and pulled it over my head. "Why? I didn't realize my life was subject to being torn apart by everyone."

"Jesus, what bit your balls this morning?"

"I just want to be left alone. Yes, I stayed at Jamie's, and yes, I'm going straight to work to avoid more of this bullshit questioning. Now get out of my room before you see me naked." I unbuttoned my jeans to emphasize my point, and it was all she needed. She bolted, shutting my door behind her.

Shit, I was hungry and I needed a coffee, since I'd been forced to abandon mine.

I changed my boxers and jeans and sat down on my bed. Resting my elbows on my knees, I leaned forward, clasping my hands and staring out of the window.

Questions. So many fucking questions. I didn't need them from my family, because I had enough of my own to answer.

How did I really feel about Jamie?

That was the prevailing one. That was the one it all boiled down to, and the one I couldn't answer, because I didn't know how to put it into words. She'd gone from being the biggest pain in my ass to a source of amusement—from that, she'd been tolerable, but now...

I wanted her around. Both in and out of my garage, and that was the terrifying thing. It'd been two weeks, and I'd sworn I wouldn't give in. I'd sworn I'd never hire her, but now, firing her seemed impossible. Not only was it cruel, it was unnecessary.

There was enough work for both of us.

She was fucking good at what she did.

And hell, I wanted her to want to be around me. I wasn't the easiest person to get along with a lot of the time, but we'd already established that to be a shared trait.

I just...wanted her.

It was that simple. I wanted her. All of her. Not just what I already had. I wanted more of her.

Whatever it meant.

I grabbed my stuff from the bed and headed downstairs. I knew my sister would be in the kitchen, with Charley already on the bus to school at this time. Pops would still be sleeping, and Greta had likely gone back to bed because, well, this was too early for her to be awake.

I was right. It was completely silent except for the clink of Roxy's spoon against the side of her bowl. She ignored me steadfastly as I moved to the coffee machine. Even when I glanced over at her, she never looked up from scrolling down her phone.

Guilt settled in. I'd let my frustration over my own inner thoughts get the better of me.

I finished making my coffee and sat down with her. "I'm sorry, Rox."

She finally looked up at me. "Don't be. I deserved it. You're clearly in a bad mood."

"Well, that's what happens when you get caught half-naked in someone's daughter's kitchen."

Her eyebrows shot up. "Her dad?"

"Her mom. Thank God." I explained the awkward encounter and how I'd escaped further questioning, but probably set myself up to feel Jamie's wrath.

She laughed. "Then you're definitely forgiven. Ouch. She's going to kick your ass."

I nodded with a grimace. "Yeah. But I couldn't just stay there, you know? I had to run."

"You're such a pussy."

"Shut up. It was awkward. She knew what had happened and, yeah."

"What did happen?"

"I confused myself," I admitted. "And I have no idea how she feels."

Roxy pushed her phone to the side. "Are you admitting you have feelings for her?"

"There's no need to look so shocked. I am capable of emotion, you know."

"I know, but you two..." She paused. "Actually, now that I think about it, you make perfect sense."

"I guess I have feelings for her. I don't really know how to put it in a box. I just know that... I don't know."

"I know." Her lips twitched up. "You smile a lot when you talk about her. Even now, and I bet you don't even realize it."

I covered my mouth with my hands. Shit, she was right. I was smiling.

"See? And, in the nicest possible way, you've been obsessed with her ever since you hired her. You've spoken about her just about every day, so I'm really not surprised that you're falling in love with her."

"Wait. I didn't say I was falling in love with her."

My sister propped her head up on her hand and said, "You don't have to, Dex. It's written all over your face."

# 27

## JAMIE

"How could you!" I shouted it before I'd even stepped foot in the garage. "How could you leave me alone with her?"

Dex jumped, banging his head on a car hood. "Hi to you, too."

I tossed my purse to the side. "Don't you "hi" me, Dexter Ryne! You left me alone with my mother!"

He turned around, rubbing his hand across the back of his head. "The horror."

"Don't start with that!" I stalked across the garage and jabbed my finger against his chest. "You know exactly what I'm talking about, you little shit."

"Hey, hey! That hurts!" He grabbed my wrist.

"Good!" I jabbed him with my other hand. "Maybe you know how painful that conversation was after you ran out on me!"

He grabbed my other wrist and met my eyes.

"I didn't run out on you. I had to get ready for work. You know that."

"Oh, cut the bullshit," I snapped. "You knew exactly what you were doing, and if I were a smarter woman, I'd have left with you to avoid that sweet hell!"

"It's good to know we're both traumatized by the events of this morning."

"She asked me why you ran off. And I said, "Gee, Mom, maybe because you let yourself into my house and walked in on him practically naked?" and she didn't see the problem. She didn't see it, Dex!" I paused. "Can you let me go?"

He cast his gaze over my face. "No, I don't think so. I think you might hurt yourself."

I was pretty incensed.

"Then she shouted at me—at me!—because I demanded to take her key back and kicked her out."

"You took back her key?"

"I forced her to give it back," I corrected. "I told her that if she didn't, next time, I'd make sure you were completely naked."

"Next time!"

"If I forgive you for running out and leaving me to explain to my mother why the man who was naked in my kitchen is my boss!" I wrestled my hands free and smacked his chest.

Dex laughed and grabbed my hands again, this time linking his fingers between mine. "Well, if it helps, Aunt Greta was waiting for me at the front door and interrogated me."

"Not at all."

"My sister bugged the hell out of me."

"I'd feel better if she didn't do that on a daily basis."

"I'm not going to get forgiven for this, am I?"

I stared at him. "There's literally nothing you can do to make me feel better about the fact you abandoned me." I pulled back from him, but his grip on my hands was too strong, and he pulled me right back against his body.

"Go to reception and look on the counter," he said in a low voice.

I jerked back. "What? Why?"

"Don't argue. Just do it."

I eyed him for a moment, then pulled my hands out of his. He let me go, and I stared at him suspiciously before finally dragging my eyes away from him and walking into reception.

A large, brown envelope was sitting on the computer keyboard. My name was scrawled on the front in blocky capitals, and I picked the envelope up with a frown. It wasn't particularly heavy or thick.

What the hell was inside?

I flipped it over to find that the flap was open. I hesitated for a second before I opened it and pulled the contents out halfway.

### *CONTRACT OF EMPLOYMENT*

I dropped the envelope on the desk like it was on fire.

Was that—did that say what I thought it did?

I snatched it back up and looked. Yep. It did. It was a contract of employment.

And I was so confused.

I carried it back through to the workshop where Dex was waiting and staring at me already. "What is this?" I held it up.

He wiped his face with his shirt. "Exactly what it says it is."

"Contract of employment? You're hiring me?"

"I'm not firing you."

"Is this how you're going to get me to forgive you for abandoning me?"

"Wait, what?" He frowned, then his eyebrows shot up. "No—shit, no. The timing is a bit weird, I get it, but it's coincidence, I promise."

I frowned, looking at it and then back to him. "It's not been three weeks."

"I don't think you need three weeks." He held his hands out. "You proved me wrong. You belong here. Maybe more than I do."

My heart thumped, and I looked down at the sheets in my hand. "Really?"

"Jamie." Dex walked toward me and cupped my cheek. "I want you to work here. I want you to *want* to work here. I promise it's just that simple. It has nothing to do with anything other than that."

"I don't know. I—"

"Cross my heart," he said softly.

I opened my mouth but closed it again. I knew he was being honest. Those were his magic words, after all.

"Okay." I smiled up at him.

He smiled right back.

"But I'm still not forgiving you for running out on me."

He dropped his hand and groaned. "And here I was hoping you might take mercy on me."

I slid the contract back inside the envelope, folded it, and whacked his arm with it. "No mercy. I might never forgive you for it."

"Would another orgasm help?"

"Doesn't this," I waved the contract, "stop any inappropriateness?"

Dex snatched it off me. "Let me go rewrite that."

I took it right back. "Nope. I saw something about tacos. I don't want you to accidentally take that back. I can live without shenanigans."

"Do you actually think I'd remove your right to have tacos twice a week for lunch? I'd be taking away my own. That would be counterproductive."

"Twice a week, huh? Who's driving to get them?"

"Both of us. We go once a week."

I tilted my head to the side. "I'll let you add in shenanigans if you do both the taco trips."

He stared at me. "Man, you drive a hard bargain."

"You can't have everything."

"You're the one who gets shenanigans and doesn't have to drive to the next town over to get tacos twice a week."

"And I'll forgive you for abandoning me."

"For the last time, I didn't abandon you. And I got my own ass-kicking from my aunt."

I folded my arms. "My mother saw you pretty much naked. That means I win."

He groaned and held out a hand. "Fine. I'll write that all in."

I handed it to him. "Thank you." I waited until he was basically in the staff room before I said, "And, by the way, my mother wants to talk to you."

"Wait, what?"

"Oh, shit. Is that the phone?" I ran to reception where I knew it wasn't ringing.

"Jamie! Goddamn it!"

Revenge was a dish best served...well, usually cold, but this was red-hot.

And so, so satisfying.

---

"And what, exactly, are your intentions with my daughter?"

Dex blinked at my father. "I'm sorry, sir?"

Dad quirked an eyebrow. "You hired her past the trial today, did you not?"

"Yes. I did."

I hid my smile behind my hand and scratched beneath Barbie's ear with the other.

"Well? What are your intentions? Is this full-time? Will she get freedom in the garage?"

Dex visibly relaxed. "It'll be a continuation of

what she's been doing for the past two weeks."

"Which is?"

"Kicking his ass," I replied.

"Yeah," Dex agreed. "That's pretty much as close as we're gonna get to the truth."

Dad looked at me with a smile. "That's my girl."

I returned the smile with a grin of my own. "Like you'd ever doubt that."

"Of course not. But it's nice to see you with someone who seems like a decent guy and obviously respects you."

Now. Respects me now. But better late than never, right?

"Oh." Mom's voice came from the doorway. "So, you told your father you're seeing each other?"

And just like that, you could hear a pin drop.

No, seriously, my dad even muted the TV.

Dex stared at me. I met his eyes briefly before looking at my mom. She still had her floral oven mitts on her hands.

"Mom," I said wearily.

"Who's seeing who?" asked Dad.

Mom started speaking before I could say a word. "I went to see Jamie this morning and young Dex here was a...visitor."

I scooped Barbie off my lap onto the cushion next to me. "I knew this was a bad idea. I knew it."

"Jamie—"

"Mrs. Bell, do you mind if I go?" I heard Dex

ask before I slammed the back door.

I stepped out onto the porch and zipped up my sweater. I'd only gone along with my mom's idea for dinner because I never expected her to blurt that out.

And, I mean, technically, we weren't seeing each other. Not officially. Not really. I'd certainly never said anything like that to make her feel like we were.

Right now, as far as I was concerned, we were two people who were attracted to each other, who happened to work together, and who happened to act on that attraction a couple times.

It didn't really matter if I got butterflies whenever our eyes met or if my stomach flipped every time he touched me. It didn't matter at all that my heart beat crazy fast more often than it was normal when it was around.

And it most definitely didn't matter that there was nothing better than falling asleep in his arms last night.

And because of all that, it really, really didn't matter that my feelings toward him had changed from something twisted and angry to something softer and more consuming than anything I'd ever felt.

No, it didn't matter at all.

Not even a little bit.

"Jamie?" Dex stepped out onto the porch.

I looked back at him but said nothing, wrapping my arms around my waist.

The door clicked shut and he came to stand

next to me. Nudging me with his elbow, he leaned in slightly and said, "Hey. I don't think I mix well with your family."

I quietly laughed and dipped my face down to look at the ground. "I don't mix well with my family. I'm sorry."

"What for?"

"My mom. If you want to go...Nobody would blame you."

"Nah, you're all good. After all, everything happens in threes. I figure she's already embarrassed me twice today, so what's one more time?"

I groaned and looked over at him. "Don't tempt fate. Please. This has been bad enough."

He put his hands in his pockets. "Well, if it makes a difference, your dad was more annoyed that your mom has been meddling than anything else."

"It's a habit." I moved back to sit on the swinging seat.

Dex joined me. "Yeah. I got that from the whole salt and sugar story thing."

I let go of a little laugh and leaned right back. "My God. She's the worst. She's so embarrassing. I don't even know why she said that. I didn't tell her a thing this morning and—"

Resting one arm on the back of the chair, he hooked one finger beneath my chin and turned my head so our eyes met. "Does it matter?"

"Does what matter?"

"What she said. Do you care?"

"Of course, I care. I mean—"

"Why? Why do you care?"

I swallowed, looking into his bright yet gentle eyes. "Because," I said softly. "I don't even—I don't even know what's happening right now. And she just blurts it out."

He released my chin to push my hair from my face. "I get it."

"And you offer me the job at a really coincidental time, and I know you weren't lying, but it feels weird, and then my mom—"

Dex dipped his head and pressed his lips to mine to shut me up. "I know it looks that way," he said in a low voice. "But I swear to you, Jamie, it's not. The way I feel about you has nothing to do with me hiring you."

He froze as if he realized what he just said.

"The way you...feel about me?" I swallowed, leaning back. "Which is...what?"

"I..." He hesitated before he ran his fingers through my hair. "I want you, Jamie. Every way I can have you. I don't know how else to say it."

I smiled and tilted my face down. My cheeks burned, but there was no denying the thrill that danced through me at his words. I didn't know how I'd come to this point, but we had.

Two weeks wasn't long, but I knew, categorically, I felt something for this man. Something very, very real. Something that had crept up between the arguments and the bickering and the kissing.

It didn't matter that I'd only just really

recognized it.

The one thing I didn't need was my mother doing so before I did.

"Well, I guess that's okay," I muttered.

"Okay? What do you mean, okay?" He sank his fingers into my hair and tugged my head back.

I grinned.

"You're a pain in the ass," he said, closing the distance between our mouths until our lips touched. It was barely a brush, but it tingled across my skin all the same.

"I'm not going to let up on you, you know. I'm still going to kick your ass all the time." I rested my head on his shoulder.

"I wouldn't expect anything less. But at least I can smack your ass now."

"Is that right?"

Dex looped his arm around my body and linked his fingers together, resting his head on top of mine. "I'll let you smack mine right back."

I snorted. "Done."

"Should we go inside and explain ourselves to your parents?"

"Nah. Let my mom stew."

The back door opened right as I said that, and I jolted upright. It was Dad, and he pulled the door almost closed. His gaze darted between the two of us, and a smile tugged at his lips.

"I guess you're going to let your mother think about what she said," he said, letting his smile grow.

I grinned and leaned back into Dex.

Dad saluted and walked back inside, letting the door click shut.

Dex kissed my forehead, and I knew that somehow...

I'd won.

# *Epilogue*

## DEX

*Two months later*

"It's your turn to get the tacos."

"No, we made a deal last night. I cooked, so you said you'd get tacos today."

"No, I didn't. I had my fingers crossed behind my back, so it doesn't count."

Sasha, our new, nineteen-year-old apprentice looked between us. "Do you two ever not fight?"

Jamie grimaced and looked at her. "Would you believe we were way worse than this when we met? We couldn't stand each other."

"I can't imagine anything worse than this," she said.

"Oh, it's true. We would fight all the time, but somehow, I charmed her into falling in love with me." I flashed Jamie a grin.

"Charmed? More like you tricked me. Somewhere between tacos and fighting and your aunt getting me drunk."

"I'm just—I'm gonna get the phone." Sasha covered her mouth with her hand, but her laughter was obvious as she darted through the workshop to get to the phone.

I moved closer to Jamie and took the wrench from her. I'd quickly learned—not long after we'd made our relationship official—that her temper was a very real thing.

The standing toolbox I'd once fucked her up against had the dent to prove it.

She'd been restricted on tools for a while.

"Look, if you still can't tell Aunt Greta no when she's got a tray full of whiskey shots..."

She pointed her finger at me. "Tell that to your sister. She's a damn bad influence on me."

"No, she's a pusher, and you give in to her. You've literally been arguing with me about who's getting tacos for lunch for fifteen minutes, yet she bats her eyelashes at you, and the next thing I know, I'm carrying you to bed."

She sniffed and folded her arms. "At least I didn't throw up on you again."

"And you're still getting tacos because I cooked you dinner last night."

"No, you cooked us dinner. That's what happens when you infiltrate your girlfriend's house to the point you live together."

I pretended to be shocked. "Infiltrated your house? I'm offended. Besides, you stayed at my place one time and got grilled by Greta about sex the next day although we were both too afraid to do anything."

"I'm not saying I mind—"

"You like that I infiltrated your house?"

"You just said you didn't!"

"Oh God, you're still going?" Sasha came back into the workshop. "I have an idea. I know the taco place. Why don't you give me money and I'll go get lunch so you can both finish your freaky foreplay?"

I turned to her, blinking. "One, I let my sister spend way too much time around you people. And two, why the hell can I not hire a nice, quiet, sass-less woman?"

Jamie touched her hand to my arm. "You bring out the sasshole in all of us, honey. It's really not our faults. It's all you."

I gave her a withering look before turning back to Sasha. "Go and take fifty bucks out of the register. That should cover all three of us."

"You don't need to tell me twice." Sasha grabbed her purse and threw a wave over her shoulder. "I'll go out the front."

"Ooh, big spender," Jamie teased when she'd gone.

I held a finger to my lips. "Watch it. You're getting on my nerves, woman."

"You're always on my nerves, Dex. You're practically a medical condition at this point."

"Don't you have work to do?"

"I do, but as you know by now, fucking with you is so much more fun."

I grunted and pulled her against me, sliding

my hands down her back to cup her ass. "Watch it. There aren't many places in this garage that haven't seen me fuck you yet. I'm happy to tick the rest off the list."

She eased her hands up my chest and linked her fingers behind my neck. "Why? Does it still turn you on when I give you attitude?"

"I'm pretty sure that's the reason I started seeing you as more than a gnat-like annoyance."

"Funny. It was your cock that made me realize that's exactly what you are."

"Watch your mouth, you." I grazed my teeth over her lower lip. "Or Sasha is gonna come back to something highly inappropriate."

"You already exhausted your shenanigans allowance on her day off."

"I'm the boss." I kissed along her jaw. "I can do what I want."

"You think you're the boss. We both know I'm really the one in charge."

My cock agreed, but my mind did not. "Whatever you say, darlin'."

"You're starting to piss me off, Dex."

"Awesome. I love angry sex with you. My back doesn't, but it can deal with it."

She smacked her hands against my chest and glared at me. "Dexter."

I spun us so she had her back up against my Dodge. I really needed to get it out of the garage, but for now. "Talking of the places I haven't had you yet...Over the hood of this Dodge is one of them."

She raised an eyebrow. "I don't see you wearing a wiper blade costume."

I burst out laughing, releasing her to flatten my hands on the hood of the car. "Shit. I have to order it. Can I owe you that one?"

Jamie laughed and cupped my face with her hands. "Oh, you owe me that. You have no idea how much you owe me it."

I grinned as she kissed me, and my hands slid down to her thighs. I gripped her tightly and pushed her up onto the hood of the truck.

Jamie slid her fingers through my hair and smiled down at me. "I love you, you crazy little shit."

Again, I grinned, running my eyes over her. From that frizzy hair to those mesmerizing eyes and those perfectly red lips.

To the honesty I saw shining in her eyes.

"I love you, too, Little Miss Mechanic."

*The End*

# About the Author

**Emma Hart is the** *New York Times and USA Today bestselling author of over thirty novels and has been translated into several different languages.*

She is a mother, wife, lover of wine, Pink Goddess, and valiant rescuer of wild baby hedgehogs.

Emma prides herself on her realistic, snarky smut, with comebacks that would make a PMS-ing teenage girl proud.

Yes, really. She's that sarcastic.

You can find her online at:
www.emmahart.org
www.facebook.com/emmahartbooks
www.instagram.com/EmmaHartAuthor
www.pinterest.com/authoremmahart

Alternatively, you can join her reader group at http://bit.ly/EmmaHartsHartbreakers.

You can also get all things Emma to your email inbox by signing up for Emma Alerts*. http://bit.ly/EmmaAlerts

*Emails sent for sales, new releases, pre-order availability, and cover reveals. Each cover reveal contains an exclusive excerpt.

# Books By Emma Hart

**The Vegas Nights series:**
Sin
Lust

**Stripped series:**
Stripped Bare
Stripped Down

**The Burke Brothers:**
Dirty Secret
Dirty Past
Dirty Lies
Dirty Tricks
Dirty Little Rendezvous

**The Holly Woods Files:**
Twisted Bond
Tangled Bond
Tethered Bond
Tied Bond
Twirled Bond
Burning Bond
Twined Bond

**By His Game series:**
Blindsided
Sidelined
Intercepted

**Call series:**
Late Call
Final Call

His Call

**Wild series:**
Wild Attraction
Wild Temptation
Wild Addiction
Wild: The Complete Series

**The Game series:**
The Love Game
Playing for Keeps
The Right Moves
Worth the Risk

**Memories series:**
Never Forget
Always Remember

**Standalones:**
Blind Date
Being Brooke
Catching Carly
Casanova
Mixed Up
Miss Fix-It
Miss Mechanic
The Upside to Being Single
Golden Girl (coming March 13, 2018)
The Hook-Up Experiment (coming May 8, 2018)
The Dating Experiment (coming July 24, 2018)

EMMA HART

38092519R00175

Made in the USA
Middletown, DE
05 March 2019